The Earl and His Virgin Countess

House of Lords Book 3

1Night Stand series

By
Dominique Eastwick

Copyright © 2016 by Dominique Eastwick
ISBN: 978-1-61333-980-0
Cover art by Cora Graphics

Published by Decadent Publishing Company, LLC
Look for us online at:
www.decadentpublishing.com

Praise for *The Earl & His Virgin Countess*

Ms. Eastwick has another home run with The Early and His Virgin Countess. She effortlessly blends history, romance and plot beautifully and yet makes it fresh and fun. ~ Got Romance Reviews

I give this book 5 stars. It was more than I was expecting and I look forward to reading more from this author. I find myself smiling every time I think about this book. ~ Drue's Random Chatter's Reviews

This story has some laugh out loud moments and enough intrigue to keep you reading until the end. I really hope that this will not be the last book in the series. Madame Eve should continue to do business with the ton, in my opinion. ~ Amazon Reviewer

~A Note from the Author~

Dear Reader,

There wasn't originally supposed to be a *House of Lords* series and Andrew was never meant to have a story. In fact, he didn't even have a name in the first book because *The Duke and the Virgin* was supposed to be a stand alone. But at some point I started thinking and asking myself who were the men of the poker game? And what if they all needed Madame Eve's magic touch?

Happy Reading!

Dom

Dedication

Dedicated to all the readers who take the journey with me in every book I write and every book they read.

Special thanks to Val and Kate for pulling the very best from me, Lisa for being understanding and believing in my work, and to Dawn, Tam, Emmeline, Dwayne, Trish, Tracy, and Patty for always loving me.

As always, thank-you to Nadine, who always pushes me to stop procrastinating.

Chapter One

The Duke of Foxhaven's Masquerade Ball

Even in the dull flicker of candlelight, the domino Andrew wore could not hide his well-defined features, strong jaw, and sculpted cheekbones like those found on Greek marble statutes at the British Museum. Hope swelled deep within Miranda as she took a step toward him. Years had passed since she had been so close to him. She had often spotted him in the distance when he rode through town, and, like all of those times, his gaze passed over her. But, then, it would; to him, she was simply a name. A name on a contract.

Why she let his dismissal of her upset her every time, she didn't know. Theirs was to be an arranged marriage, an arrangement between two families. She'd grown up more than aware there would be no love match for her, but one would think, in the last twenty years, his lordship could have taken the time even once to visit his future countess. Perhaps have sent a gift on her birthday or offered to escort her when she had been presented to the regent upon her coming out.

She hadn't had a season, hadn't needed one since she had already been betrothed. Unfortunately, knowing that hadn't kept her heart from yearning. Miranda wanted to go to parties; she wanted the thrill of someone signing her dance card. Hell, she wanted to feel what it was like to be a part of his world. Instead, she'd been kept in the country to learn her French, perfect the pianoforte, practice her numbers, and prepare to run her future husband's household. Only one word described her life: boring.

When the invitation inviting her to the masquerade ball had come, it had been an opportunity she would not pass up. No one could identify Miranda, and it gave her a chance to observe Andrew from afar, as always, or perhaps she might actually approach him for once. So far, however, he hadn't done anything of note. He'd strolled around, chatted briefly with a few people. And other than the tall man who commanded the room—who she assumed had to be the infamous Duke of Foxhaven—no one had held Andrew's attention longer than a moment. He had glanced at his watch twice in as many minutes, and, if she planned to make a move, she didn't have any time to lose.

But why did it feel her feet were nailed to the floor? Why would walking across the room to a man she'd spent countless years training to be a perfect wife for frighten her? Because, although she had been trained to please him in almost every way, it terrified her he would find her wanting.

He chose that very moment to look up and meet her gaze. Damn. Caught staring, she averted her eyes. Steadying herself, she looked up again to find him gone. Of course he had taken off, since an insane Little Red Riding Hood had stared at him like he was the Big Bad Wolf. Convinced her life couldn't get any more disappointing, Miranda went in search of her Aunt Sarah and then to call the carriage to take her home. The following day, Miranda would send a note to her brother, informing him she would be returning to the country house, where she would simply go back to waiting for her fiancé to claim her. She certainly wasn't about to introduce herself now.

"Where are you running to, Red?" Andrew's voice washed over her, forcing her to stop. "Heading to Grandma's house?"

She faced her earl. "No, my aunt's." *Does he recognize me?*

"Must you leave? The ball is only beginning."

Silly how her nerves acted up when she had the one thing she'd wanted for years—his undivided attention. "I should check on her."

"I am sure your aunt is having a fine time and not ready to depart yet." He took her gloved hand in his and brought it to his lips. "Why not take a stroll in the gardens with me first?"

She bit her lip. A proper lady never went anywhere with a gentleman, but he was her betrothed and therefore they were granted some freedoms most couples weren't. Even if he didn't appear to have the slightest idea of who she was, yet. "That sounds wonderful, milord."

"Follow me." He placed her hand in the crook of

4

his arm. "This way. There is a side entrance to the gardens."

If Miranda needed to find her way back, she would be out of luck, for her attention rested squarely on the man next to her rather than the hallways and rooms they passed through.

"You seem familiar with this house," she said.

The earl nodded. "His grace is one of my closest friends. I spent most of my younger years here, as his mother and mine were best friends." His smile lit his face and sent warmth to places a lady shouldn't think about, and Miranda was glad the rooms were dark enough to hide the heat on her face. Her embarrassment faded as they exited the house, however, when the fragrance of the rose garden filled her nose. Chinese lanterns draped from poles around the immaculate plot cast a pale light over the grounds. "It is beautiful."

"You are seeing her grace at her best."

"The duke's wife?

"No, Wolfe has not fallen into the parson's trap yet. His mother lives to entertain, and this is all her doing. You aren't from town, are you?" Even the half mask couldn't hide his questioning glance.

Miranda wanted to scream then remembered she wore a mask as well and he couldn't possibly recognize who she was. Ignoring the question, she asked, "Is that a hedge maze?"

"It is. Do you want to go in?"

Oh yes, she loved them. She had been through the one on his grounds several times while visiting them years before. "Is it as difficult as the one at your country estate?"

Andrew stopped to gaze upon her. Really look at her, before cocking his head as if trying to determine her identity. "You've made me."

"Yes, I know who you are." Years of training had made her the expert on the man, yet standing while he investigated every inch of her exposed face made her nervous.

"And you've been to my family estate?"

"It's been a while, but yes."

"Were you a guest at one of my house parties?"

Grinding her teeth, she prayed for strength to

prevent her anger from surfacing. "I have never been invited to one of your house parties, but I was invited to many of your celebrations."

While his mother had still been alive, she'd hosted elaborate all-day celebrations each summer, which everyone from town and the estate would be invited to enjoy. The grounds would be filled with people laughing and eating. Jugglers and puppeteers entertained the children, while the adults played croquet or sailed on the lake. The countess, though warm and welcoming, had always been cold and unapproving of Miranda. She'd never understood exactly why, but, in her soul she'd worried she hadn't measured up, which pushed her to work with her tutors until she did everything without fault.

"It's been a great many years since we hosted one of those," he said thoughtfully.

"Yes." Then, wishing to divert him, she asked, "So about this maze?"

"Hmm—oh yes, the maze. This one is more complicated than the one at my family estate, but I used to do it blindfolded. Anything to keep life

7

exciting, I guess." He pulled her behind him into the hedges, which stood two feet above Andrew's head on either side. Meticulously trimmed bushes rose high on either side of them as they progressed farther into the maze. The lights from the lanterns faded, leaving only the moonlight to help them find their way. The darker it became, the closer she pressed against him, as he led her deeper.

"Almost there," he said, his steps never faltering or pausing at any turn. In fact, with every navigation, his confident pace increased. Arriving at the center, the destination of their walk, she heard conversation.

Soft, feminine words floated through the hedge. "You're smiling."

A man responded, his words gruff and deep, "I'm happy, for more reasons than you can imagine. Shall we announce our impending wedding?"

"No, let's surprise everyone," the woman replied.

Andrew put a finger to his lips. "It appears we were about to interrupt a marriage proposal."

"Shouldn't we leave them be?" Miranda asked in a hushed voice, barely silencing a giggle.

Andrew paused. "Oh hell, I recognize that voice." Releasing her hand, he headed for the opening, with Miranda following.

The couple started at the interruption, and the gentleman stepped forward to protect his apparent fiancée. "Andrew?"

Andrew led Miranda around the hedge, out of site of the clandestine couple. "Stay here, please," he whispered, before heading back to speak with his friends.

"What the hell are you doing out here?" Miranda heard Andrew ask.

"Looking for some privacy," his acquaintance, clearly put out, replied, seemingly unaware of Miranda's presence as she peeked through leaves to watch.

"So I see." Andrew motioned to the couple. "Good evening, Mrs. Mallory."

"Lord Windenshire." The seductive voice of the woman almost purred.

"You two know each other?" his friend demanded, and Miranda didn't wait to hear Andrew's answer.

She headed back in the direction they'd come, unwilling to eavesdrop, and, for some reason, afraid to ascertain how well he knew that Mrs. Mallory. It only took a few turns before Miranda became hopelessly lost however.

Ripping off her hood, but leaving the mask on, she sat on the ground. Voices mumbled in the distance, and she stared up at the sky. The stars twinkled far less in London than at home. How she wished to be there.

Andrew appeared. "Here you are. I wondered where you'd gone." He extended a hand. "Apparently, my presence is required for a wedding tomorrow."

She glanced up at him. "Tomorrow? How is that possible?"

"An eager groom who procured a special license already. Why did you wander off?"

"I wanted to give you some privacy."

"Interesting. Most women would have used the moment to cause a stir and catch themselves a lord."

Catch a lord? Anger rose within her. "I have no interest in trapping anyone."

"Obviously not, as you didn't use the moment to your advantage."

Ignoring his hand, she stood. "Would you be so kind as to help me out of the maze? I need to check on my aunt."

"Of course." He gestured for her to follow him. As before, he navigated the rows of manicured bushes without hesitation. "Are you staying 'til midnight for the unmasking?"

"Is that what happens?" Miranda shook her head. "I don't think I want to reveal who I am to everyone."

"No?" Andrew paused at the maze entrance. "You came out with the Big Bad Wolf. You can't be scared of anything as slight as taking off your mask."

"Scared, no. I simply have no interest in the ton discovering who I am." But fear hadn't played into her decision. She gnawed on her lip. In the moonlight, she looked over his face, his well-chiseled chin with the slight appearance of stubble, the aristocratic nose, and then into his eyes. "Is that what you are? The Big

Bad Wolf?"

He touched his nose. "My nose seems normal enough. So, Red, if you won't allow me the pleasure of seeing your face at the strike of twelve, pray tell me your name."

"Miranda Beauchamp." She waited for any sort of response at his discovery that he stood before his future wife.

Instead, he smiled. "Pleasure to meet you. Shall I return you to your aunt?"

"That's all?" She prayed her voice didn't sound as shrill to his ears as it did to hers. The contents of her stomach churned, and her mouth began to water. The world spun briefly, nearly leaving her unable to catch her footing. Nothing on the earl's face gave any recognition to the name. Deep within her, red-hot anger and hurt began to build.

"I beg your pardon?"

"Does my name mean nothing to you?" she demanded rather loudly, and, when he stepped back as if she were from Bedlam, her blood boiled.

He couldn't even be bothered to remember the

name of his betrothed? She balled her hand in a fist. His words of appeasement fell from his lips upon her deaf ears. Years of frustration and loneliness surfaced.

Without thought, she let the fist make contact with his flawless nose. "You son of a donkey's ass." Running into the ballroom, all she craved was the solitude of her bed and a large, steaming cup of chocolate.

***

"What in the bloody hell happened to you?"

Not the greeting Andrew, Earl of Windenshire, expected upon arriving at the London home of his friend, Lord Simon Winston. But the last twenty-four hours could be described as anything but expected.

"A masked lady with a wicked jab caught me off guard."

Simon leaned in for a better view of Andrew's black-and-blue eye. "Not Little Red from the maze last night?"

He shifted uncomfortably under the inspecting gaze. "Yes, the very one."

With a whistle, Simon touched the edge of the bruise. "That is impressive."

Wolfe, Duke of Foxhaven, whom Andrew hadn't even realized stood nearby, peered over Simon's shoulder. "Interesting. I can see Railey inducing fits of violence in a woman, but I never imagined it your style. Speaking of the viscount, where is he?"

Simon made to touch Andrew's face again. "I saw him briefly last night at the ball, but couldn't track him down on such short notice."

Swiping at Simon's hand to prevent him from probing the foul eye again, Andrew snapped, "Do you mind? That hurts, you git."

Put out, Simon lowered his hand, but didn't back up. "What the hell did you do to irritate her?"

"Apparently, I should have claimed a familiarity with the woman, but did not. In her fit of vapors at my insult, she decided to call forth her inner Gentleman Jackson."

"Well done, indeed."

"And the lady with the iron fist. What's her name, so if I should see her in the ring, I will place my wager on her?" Wolfe chuckled. *Damn him.*

Andrew groaned. He had to own up to one of the most embarrassing parts of the situation. "That is the strange thing; I can't remember. I have tried to recall the moments about the event, but to no avail. The name is there, but as if in a fog, I can't make out."

Patting him on the shoulder, Simon chuckled. "She hit you harder than you thought if she has addled your brain so. Wolfe, do you remember that time Lord Tenley got punched at Eton so hard he didn't remember his own name or who hit him? Eventually his name came back, but he never did remember the fight."

"Gentlemen, there is a wedding to attend to.... Oh dear! Can you even see out of that eye, milord?" A blonde woman Andrew didn't recognize placed her hand on Wolfe's shoulder. The intimacy of the gesture wasn't lost on Andrew, even with damaged vision. "Perhaps a poultice would be called for. After Simon's vows, I would be happy to make one for

15

you."

Like a dog with a bone and unable to let it go, Simon asked, "Are you sure a woman did this?"

Andrew narrowed his good eye. "I was there. I assure you, she was a woman."

"I want to meet her trainer." Wolfe laughed and lifted the feminine hand on his shoulder to his lips before placing it in the crook of his arm. "Andrew, I don't think you have had the pleasure to meet Lady Elizabeth Hamilton—Llysa, my future duchess."

"It's a pleasure, milady." His bow, normally graceful and low, had to be cut short by the pounding behind his eye. In the course of twenty-four hours, two of his closest friends had fallen to the parson's trap. Yet Andrew'd had no idea either had been interested in, let alone courted, a woman. The adoration plain to see in both his grace and Llysa showed theirs was not an arranged marriage, and Andrew suspected they knew each other far better than they should.

"Lord Windenshire, it a pleasure to meet another of Wolfe's friends. I am sure we will be seeing much of you after the wedding." Her attention remained on Wolfe, the pure love and joy brightening the room before she turned her attention to Simon. "Simon, your bride is ready."

"Time to get your leg shackled," Wolfe added, but his gaze focused on Llysa.

"Happily." Simon headed for the door then paused. "Andrew, in the left-hand drawer of my desk is a writing set. Can you bring it so we can sign the marriage registry for the clergyman?"

Waving them off, Andrew approached the opulent baroque-style desk at the far end of the room. He opened the drawer, pulled out the quill set, but with his perception off, managed to brush quite a few papers to the floor. Crouching, he ignored the throb in his head and collected the scattered pages. An expensive envelope with a deep red wax seal caught his attention. Though broken, the embossed E on the seal stood out. He placed the letter back on the table and the name on the envelope jumped out at him. Madame Evangeline.

Leaning back on his heel, he glanced through the

open doors to the other room. Simon stood before the parson with his bride at his side. Next to him, Wolfe played second, his attention moving back and forth from the clergyman to Simon's fiancée on the other side of Chandra, herself soon to be the new Marchioness of Breckinridge.

Two lords, both engaged within a short time, and at least one had acquired the services of the elusive and expensive 1Night Stand service. Andrew suspected Wolfe had, too. If one had enough money and was in need of a discreet liaison for a night, no one did a better job of arranging one than Madame Evangeline. Not that Andrew knew much more about the secretive woman than a reputation only whispered about, other than her uncanny ability to bring two people together for an unforgettable evening that often went beyond that night. Since first learning about the woman a few weeks prior at a weekly poker game with the other lords, he had let curiosity get the better of him. Unfortunately, not many would admit to contacting Madame Evangeline, let alone using her services. But the few who did said she was the best.

Picking up the card that had fallen out of the envelope, he pocketed it. Since his friend obviously no longer needed it.

After making sure he'd put everything back in its rightful place, Andrew joined the wedding party in the other room. With the previous night's ordeal still fresh in his mind, perhaps he should follow Simon's lead, stop trying to find a woman within the ton, and let a professional handle it for him.

Eventually, luck had to be on his side.

Right?

***

Tears flowed, but whether from the pain in her knuckles, or the sadness in her heart, Miranda couldn't say. After arriving alone back at her aunt's house, she'd spent the rest of the evening under the covers, crying into her pillows in hopes no one would hear her. Embarrassed and feeling betrayed, she didn't think she could handle the servants' gossip as well. Since Miranda had snuck off the night before with Lord Windenshire into the garden, her whole sense of who she was had collapsed. Everything she had ever done or been taught had been a lie. She had wasted her life on a dream, been a naïve fool to believe what everyone told her without question.

"There you are."

"You found me." Wiping the tears from her face, Miranda smiled with what she hoped would pass as anything other than heartbreak and disillusionment under her Aunt Sarah's watchful gaze. "You're up early."

"Silly gel, I have only just arrived home." Sarah sat on the edge of the bed. "So how did your walk in the garden go?"

Easing up in the bed so her back rested against the cushioned headboard, Miranda plucked at a thread on one of her pillows. "You saw that?"

Her aunt rolled her eyes. As if Miranda could have left the ballroom without the notice of the woman. "Of course I saw it, and I would have been worried if you were in the same room with the earl and didn't take the opportunity to speak with him. I suppose you got an answer from him."

"I supposed I did."

"Well?" Aunt Sarah huffed. "Don't leave me in suspense."

"His lordship had not an inkling of who I was."

"He hasn't seen you since you were…honestly, I can't remember how old you were."

Shaking her head, Miranda pulled the quilt tighter around herself. "No. I meant he didn't know who Miranda Beauchamp was."

Sarah gave her a perplexed frown. "That can't be correct. There is a signed contract stating the two of you were betrothed as infants."

Yes, but signed when Andrew had been but a week old, and Miranda yet to be born. "Have you ever seen the contract?" she asked.

"No, but I can't imagine your mother lying about it. It made sense, and your father spoke at length that combining the two estates would lead to all those great things men care about; it would right a wrong, and other such drivel. To be honest, I rarely listened past the first few words. My brother bored saints. And

I am no saint. And, neither was your mother. She was more of a—"

Miranda had grown up hearing how despised her mother had been by anyone who knew her. "Aunt Sarah, please, not today." Changing the subject, she said, "I wonder if Daniel can locate the contract?"

"If anyone can tell us where it might be, it would be your idiot brother. Or the family solicitor here in London would surely have it. Shall I send a missive asking a representative to come meet with us?"

"Would you?"

"Of course, dear. Although I don't see what difference it might make."

It would make all the difference in the world. "I need to discern if I am free to live my life, I suppose. Am I free of my obligation to Lord Windenshire?"

"Now that is something I might be able to help you with. Are you sure you want out of the contract?"

Nodding, Miranda moved closer to her.

"Very well. The best way to get out of this marriage contract is to compromise yourself—" Aunt Sarah frowned. "Don't look at me as if you are shocked. And you can close your mouth while you are at it, not at all ladylike. If you aren't pure, no one will fight the legality of the agreement made between two foolish men. I am familiar with a woman who helps set up evenings between the well-to-do."

Miranda stopped her jaw from dropping, but only just, not sure if the shock came from her aunt being aware of such a woman, or because she spoke about it so openly with her. "How do you know of this?"

"I might be your maiden aunt, but I am no maiden. I decided years ago life would be easier without a man to be chained to, and I am one of the few women of our time blessed with freedom and money to live my life the way I choose. I, too, had an aunt once. Aunt Milly left me everything she owned so I would not need a man to be reliant upon."

"I've never heard of Milly."

"You wouldn't. My brother thought it unfair for her vast estate to go to me, a simple bluestocking. Milly's name never crossed your father's lips once she died." Sarah waved a hand. "Now back to what's important...I have actually used Madame

Evangeline's services twice. Both resulted in long-term, mutually satisfying relationships for me and the men."

"Aunt Sarah...." Miranda's cheeks burned, the heat of embarrassment threatening to engulf her. "I don't think this is a conversation we should be having."

"Don't be a ninny. Who else is going to have this talk with you? Your mother, who ran off with that officer to the wilds of Australia? Perhaps your brother. No? Darling, if you want to get yourself out of this asinine contract, then you have to do some things you might not be comfortable with. I support you either way."

"This Madame Evangeline...she won't tell anyone?"

"Strict confidence. I trust her. I wouldn't send you to anyone I didn't trust. I love you as if you were my own daughter."

"I love you the same." Sarah had been more of a mother to her than Miranda's own mother. Sarah had attended every major event in Miranda's childhood.

And, although she continued Miranda's training to be the impeccable countess, she never bit her tongue about how she felt. "How much do her services cost?"

Waving her away, her aunt approached the yellow floral brocade drapes, pulling them closed. "Consider this a gift from me. An independence party. Besides, the pittance of an allowance your brother gives you to keep you on tight reins wouldn't pay for it, even though, of course, it is your money and not his."

"I can't ask you...."

"You aren't asking, I am offering. I think this might be the best thing to ever happen to you. How long would you have waited for the earl, had your eyes not been opened? And how many young ladies has he pulled into gardens with the intention of debauching them?"

Miranda's knuckles ached, and unlike her aunt, turning away the responsibility, even one the earl didn't seem to acknowledge or care about, wasn't as easy as simply saying so. Exhaustion seeped into each and every pore.

25

"Get some sleep, Miranda. I will send a missive to Madame Eve, as well as the lawyer. But do me a favor and promise me you won't punch your date the way you obviously did the earl."

"How…?"

"Your knuckles are red and puffy, and the earl, though discreet, returned holding a bloody nose. Did you think I would allow you to stroll into a dark garden with any man, even your betrothed, and not have my eyes open for your return?" Sarah smiled then gave her a kiss on her forehead before leaving the room.

Miranda stared at the ceiling molding, then closed her eyes and prayed for a new life, whatever that new life might be. A tear fell, and she let it. It would be the last one for a life she'd thought she would have. When she woke, she would brave her new life head on. For the moment, she needed to bury her countess fantasies and face a new reality.

Chapter Two

Andrew searched the elegant rooms one at a time. The suite included a small, private dining room, bedroom with a bed that rivaled the Bed of Ware, and a bathing chamber. Checking his pocket watch, he groaned. His *companion* for the evening was now a full hour late. He'd had a feeling in his gut that from the beginning the meeting had been a bad idea.

When he opened the door, a servant stepped forward. "Milord?"

"Call for my carriage."

Bowing, the servant excused himself, right before a commotion caught Andrew's attention.

A woman's voice floated toward him. "I can walk."

He made it down to the ground floor in time to see a man in the livery of the house carrying the woman into the first sitting room. "What happened?"

"My apologies, sir. The young lady was involved in a minor accident."

"Accident." Andrew pushed past the lingering servants and looked over the scene, before his gaze rested on the new arrival. To his surprise, the beauty was both everything he'd expected and nothing. In the brief moment he'd had to hear and observe her, she'd emanated a feistiness to match her hair color. Even as she shooed away the servant who'd been trying to assess her injuries, she did so with the decorum and grace of a well-bred woman.

"Sir, remove your hand," she demanded, trying to pull her foot from the servant's grasp.

"You heard her ladyship," Andrew said. "Now, someone fetch a maid for the lady, and everyone else get out." He approached her. "Someone needs to tell me what the hell happened."

"You!" Her eyes widened with recognition. "What are you doing here?"

Something about her seemed familiar, yet he doubted he had ever seen her before. Mayhap it was her voice or the way she held herself. He could not pinpoint what it was but he *knew* he knew her. "Have we met?"

"No." she said. "You aren't the gentleman I was meeting here are you?"

A nearby maid appeared and gave him a nod.

"Apparently," he replied.

The gentlewoman addressed the maid. "There has to be a mistake."

The woman shook her head. "Mademoiselle, I apologize. It is highly unusual for a servant to see both people. But, I assure you, no one will talk. Now, allow me to assess your ankle."

She lifted the right foot, and Andrew's mouth dried as the maid raised the hem of her light-green gown to expose a dainty ankle. Unfortunately, even under her stockings, the ankle appeared swollen and bruised. "Ouch."

Andrew crouched before her and asked the maid, "Do you have any ice?"

"Oui."

"Fetch some, please."

"No!" the injured lady said. "I mean, it isn't proper for us to be left alone."

Raising an eyebrow, he tried hard not to scoff. "I

hate to bring up the obvious, but did you think there would be a maid with us the whole evening?"

"No, of course not, I thought—that is, I didn't think—it would be you."

"I see." Standing, he took a few steps back, but never took his eyes off her. What had he done to this woman for her to be so opposed to spending the evening with him? He wasn't the town's most notorious rake, and he had no recollections being with her before, at least not long enough to have offended her.

The maid returned with a bowl of ice and a cloth, and handed them to him. "Monsieur."

"Thank you. Would you have the prepared food brought into this room?"

"Yes, sir."

He placed a few chunks of ice into the cloth then, turning toward his *maiden in distress*, he asked, "Shall I place this on your ankle, or do you wish to do it yourself?" Andrew could not imagine how she planned to do it without his help.

She took a minute to debate her answer. "Would

you be so kind as to assist me?"

"I am yours to command." He smiled, her words must have tasted like crow. "So what exactly happened?"

"With the carriage, you mean?"

"Aye."

"Honestly, I can't say for sure. We hit a bump and, the next thing I knew, I was bounced into the air, and we were sitting at an odd angle. The rear wheel—" She hissed as the ice touched her stockinged leg.

"Continue," he urged, although he already had a good idea what had happened. But he wanted to take her mind off her injury.

"What—oh right, the rear wheel was in pieces, smashed beyond recognition."

"You are lucky."

"How so?"

"You might have been killed or thrown from the carriage. People have died of lesser accidents." He knew firsthand, as a cousin had died in that very manner.

The blood drained from her face, leaving a

greenish tint. Without thinking, he lifted her into his arms and walked the few steps to a nearby chaise lounge. He laid her down so her foot rested on the back and her head lay where her feet should have been.

"Do you need me to call for a maid to ease your corset ties?"

"No…maybe." She sighed. "I am not usually one to fall into vapors."

"I never thought you were." In truth, he believed she wasn't. "You have had a bit of a shock tonight. When did you last eat?"

"This morning,"

"Is the room spinning?"

"Not so bad now that I am lying down. Thank you."

"Nothing I wouldn't have done for any lady in need." He smiled. They were interrupted by a knock on the door. The maid entered then paused. "What is it?" he asked.

"The servants are uncomfortable entering when you are both present, milord. It's the policy for no one to see both persons. Tonight we have broken that rule. They—we would all like to amend that now."

"I understand. If you will leave the food on a trolley in the hall, I will bring it in. Thank you."

"Merci."

"Wait. Before you leave, let me step out so that you may help...." He paused and looked at the lady on the chaise. "It occurs to me I have yet to acquire your name."

"Miranda."

"Miss Miranda is in need of some assistance." He bowed before leaving them alone for the maid to release her stays. A butler met him as he walked out and Andrew asked, "Have you arranged for her ride home?"

"We are working on repairing the wheel. It appears to be the only damage. But that will take a few hours. We do not want to send her home in your carriage, as it's marked with your family seal, and a hackney can't guarantee secrecy."

"Understandable. The lady will also require assistance into her residence, as I do not believe she can walk on that ankle."

"We will send a servant or two to assist her."

"Very well."

The butler left him in the hall to his thoughts, Miranda being the main one. *Hell.* There were seven Mirandas of his acquaintance in the ton alone. So her name, though not as popular as some, was still common enough. And while her voice caused a sizzle of recognition, he'd never seen her face. He would have remembered her. It did seem unfortunate she knew him and hated the association. None of this helped him understand her any better.

The sitting room door opened, yet no one emerged. Pushing it wider, he spotted a hidden panel at the other end close. He lifted the tray of food off the trolley and brought it in, placing it on the table in the corner. Miranda had moved and sat on the chaise with her foot propped on a large bolster.

"Feeling better?"

She nodded. "Yes, thank you for asking."

"What can I get for you to eat? Something light, I think, easy on the stomach."

Nodding again, she shifted slightly. He imagined she was quite uncomfortable at the moment, both emotionally and physically. After filling her plate with a slice of bread and some fruit, and, pouring her a cup of tea, he considered adding a glass of wine, but decided she needed something solid first. Handing her the cup of tea, he pulled a small spindle table toward her with his free hand.

"Start with this, and if you can keep it down and want more, I can make you another plate."

Over the edge of her teacup, she looked at the table then back at him. She certainly had the grande dame haughty stare down to an art form. "I don't expect you are used to serving others."

"If you mean...." He paused to ensure she paid attention, not relishing having to explain to her again, that unlike her, acting a snob, he was anything but. *Madame Evangeline has failed miserably on this match.* "I am able to serve myself, if necessary, but I feel it's more important to put people to work. And as I can afford to pay someone to make my meals and another to serve them to me, that is two more people who can bring money home to families who need them."

A rosy flush spread across her pale skin. "I beg your pardon, milord."

"Please call me Andrew." Placing food on his plate, he filled the last empty spot with a piece of quail. He swirled the red wine in his glass and wished it were something stronger, but, in the end, alcohol in any form was welcome. Nothing about the evening could be described as planned.

"It wouldn't be proper to call you by your given name," she said.

"And I suppose coming here to meet with a strange man for a clandestine evening is proper? Did you plan to call me milord while we made use of the large bed upstairs? When you screamed your pleasure, would it be 'milord' on your lips?"

Her perfect lips formed an O and then began to tremble. *Christ, she's about to cry.* To his utter surprise, she threw her head back and laughed out loud. Not a delicate giggle, but a laugh that started from deep within and engulfed her entirely. Even

36

more surprising: she enchanted him.

Her eyes filled with tears of mirth. He hadn't taken the opportunity to truly look at her. Tears of laughter streamed down her freckled cheeks, and he gave in. Her reddish hair, a hue that would never make her the envy of the ton, fell in disarray around her delicate face, framing her green eyes. But the fiery color suited her, brought out a rose tint in her lips and cheeks that made her seem more alive.

There was no pretense to her, and certainly she had been less than impressed with him. He doubted, even were he a prince or a king, it would make any difference to her. She hadn't held back her disenchantment of him, yet apologized honestly when he'd corrected her. This Miranda intrigued him in a way he hadn't felt in a while.

"You must think me a complete prig." She wiped the tears away with the back of her hand. An action in no way *de rigueur*, but which nevertheless didn't make her appear any less ladylike.

Taking pity on her, he handed her the linen handkerchief from his inner coat pocket. "No, I think you a lady who has been through much this evening."

She snorted, wiping the tears from her eyes. "Some lady."

"You appear to be perking up."

She utterly charmed him with her unfettered enjoyment. Most women of his acquaintance only let men see them in the best light. A lady in public was always dainty and would never laugh until tears poured down her cheeks, and certainly wouldn't point out her own faults. "Perhaps you would like something more substantial to eat."

"Yes, please. Perhaps it's unladylike to admit, but I am starving."

He smiled, taking her plate. "It's actually quite refreshing. I grow tired of petite young things who eat nothing and pass out at a drop of the hat."

"I am neither young nor petite."

No, she had curves in all the right places. Making sure it wasn't ignored, his cock twitched as it hardened. "You seem perfect to me."

"Ha! Far from perfect." Again her lips formed the tantalizing O before she asked, "Did you put something in my tea?"

"I did not."

"Then I have no excuse for my behavior."

He laughed that time, filling her plate with a bit of everything. "You have done nothing in need of excusing."

"But I would have thought you'd prefer a perfect woman." Her eyes clouded with what appeared to be confusion. He supposed it wasn't too hard to believe; a peer of the realm would be looking for what society considered would be important in a mate. He handed her the plate laden with delicacies and far more food than he had ever seen any woman eat.

"Thank you, milord—Andrew."

"You're welcome. Now, indulge me." he said, retaking his seat in the high back chair. "What do you think is perfection?"

"I believe...." Taking a bite, she contemplated the question. "Perfection for you would be a woman who is well-mannered and carries herself with decorum at all times. She is the perfect hostess. She does delicate needlework, plays the pianoforte, and sings beautifully. She would complement you, if on your arm, and would never argue."

What she described sounded like a paper doll. A woman with no thoughts of her own. He didn't want a vacant vessel in his bed only for the purpose of begetting children; he wanted a partner. Andrew yearned to have a woman look at him the way Llysa and Chandra looked at their men. Both women stood up to their lordly men, all the while complementing and supporting Wolfe and Simon. "Sounds bloody boring, if you ask me."

"Really."

"Might as well be with a living statue. I'll bet this woman would also stare at the ceiling and think about England while I drive into her."

She choked on her bite. "I suppose she just might."

"And she probably eats enough to stay barely alive, ties her corset too tight, and then faints at the slightest hint of impropriety."

"Oh dear, yes, into the most dainty faints possible."

"I would rather face the guillotine than endure a woman of that sort." Setting his food aside, he turned his attention fully on her. Her face lit up as they continued to banter back and forth, showing none of the disgust she'd found for him earlier. Standing, he grabbed her plate while ignoring her protest. "Would you condemn me to such a cavernous, empty life, Miranda?"

"Condemn?"

"Utter and complete boredom." He sat on the edge of the seat next to her. "Somehow I have a feeling you could never bore me."

"Well, but then, I am not perfect."

"Perfection is in itself boring. It's our individual flaws that make us interesting, who we are. It's what the marriage-minded mamas have failed to realize when they prance their daughters out every season, like mares at Tattersales." Miranda swallowed hard when he leaned closer. "Would you condemn me to such a life?"

Miranda shook her head, eyes wide with shock and confusion. She resembled a deer caught unaware of being approached. But, unlike the poor doe, who would bolt in a second, Miranda would not. In reality, she could not walk across the room, let alone run from his embrace. Even if she could run on her injured leg, Andrew had already decided he wouldn't let her.

"Let's test that theory out," he murmured, his mouth a hairbreadth from hers. She smelled of lavender and rose petals, his favorite scent on a lady. His lips touched hers, at first a mere brush. Her eyes fluttered shut. She placed a tentative hand on his chest, fingertips light against the fabric of his shirt.

He wrapped an arm around her waist, pulling her closer. Working his tongue between her closed lips, he wanted to show her, to teach her the dance with his mouth. Her sweetness and innocence moved him. He brushed aside the thought she might be innocent and deepened the kiss. Her hand fisted the fine cloth separating them, while he gripped her arm.

He continued until her lips softened and she sighed into the kiss, and only then did he ease her into the arched back of the chaise. Shrugging out of his overcoat, he placed a knee on the cushion next to her, never breaking away from her mouth. Every inch of him burned, and he longed to see if she was as much a spitfire under the bedclothes. He loved the way her curves gave him a landscape to play on.

He grew harder, thinking about it. He had always preferred women with meat on their bones. They were softer, somehow, and he ached for her round, full thighs wrapped around him. Moaning into her mouth, he shifted to accommodate the rock-hard cock in his breeches. He began to explore the fullness of her hip before going back into the valley of her waist and uphill to her ample breasts. Though longing to taste them, he enjoyed the kiss too much to break away just yet.

Reaching one breast, Andrew cupped and kneaded it. The nipple hardened to a tight nub before Miranda pushed him firmly away, ripping her mouth from his.

"No—no, I am sorry, I can't. Not with you."

He froze, his eyes locked on hers. "Are you saying if another man were here, you'd let him?"

Anger filled him like nothing he had ever felt. She wanted *him*. But something about Lord Andrew Masterson, Earl of Windenshire, offended her. Could he make her see the man behind the title, or would she forever only see the earl?

"Milord, please move," she said, her voice small and timid.

He rose, unable to look at her, and paced around the oval table in the center of the room, to the tray of food and the bottle of wine. Pouring a glass, he downed it. "I think it's time you tell me what offense I have committed. Don't you?"

"You really have no clue?" She snorted with what sounded like disgust.

"Believe me, milady, I am not in the habit of feigning ignorance."

She began to speak then placed a hand on her lips. Whatever lurked beneath the surface, she wasn't about to share. He should walk out the door and never see the chit again. But, instead, he downed another glass of wine before holding the bottle toward her in silent inquiry. She shook her head and, since apparently she already thought the worst of him, drinking himself into a stupor wouldn't alter that. Of course, he would need more than one bottle of wine. Sitting once more, he placed his feet on the oval table with a loud thunk. He would deal with getting another bottle of wine when the one in his grip ran dry.

The heat in his gaze turned to disgust, and Miranda wondered how she had let him kiss her, let alone find her voice to tell him no. Because, even as she'd done so, the sensual side she hadn't realized existed wanted him to continue. But what happened if he found out they were betrothed? Worse, what would happen when he came to claim her as his betrothed? What would he say or do then?

The other side, her angry side, reminded her he had let her wait for years. And he had paid a great deal of money to meet with a woman for an evening of sex. Just as he had taken her out into the garden three weeks earlier, he had no intention of going to get his betrothed. He didn't care if she rotted in the country. The reasoning centered her, pushed her to tell him no, and forced her to remember who the man was.

It didn't matter that he was far too handsome for his own good. Or that the kiss had destroyed any preconceived notion she had of what their first kiss would be like. Her lips still tingled from the sensation of his hard, yet tender, lips pressing against hers. The butterflies still fluttered deep in her belly, and the tingle between her thighs had yet to subside. But he'd kissed a stranger, not his betrothed, and that hurt beyond measure.

Adjusting on the rather comfortable piece of furniture, she welcomed the pain from her ankle as it reminded her of the pain her heart had felt in the garden when he'd been unaware of her true identity. He hadn't cared what her name was. Miranda was just a faceless person his father had agreed to have him betrothed to before she was actually born.

"Are you sure you don't want any? Never let it be said I am greedy with anything involving the fairer sex," Andrew announced from across the room.

"No, milord."

"So, we are back to full propriety again, are we? Do you use the title *milord* as an insult, I wonder, or to remind yourself of who I am?"

How could she respond when she didn't have the answer? "Why did you contact Madame Eve?"

"I will answer your question if you agree to answer mine as well."

If replying to his enquiries gave her the clues she needed to move on with her life, she would play his game. She faced him, took a deep breath, and nodded. "Very well."

"Do you want the long story or a shortened version?"

"We seem to have all night." She deserved as many answers as he would give her. But her nerves tightened. Did she really want to know it all? Wasn't it better not to have her worst fears recognized? She bit her thumbnail and prepared for whatever he revealed.

He nodded. "I first heard of 1Night Stand a little over a month ago, at a poker game amongst friends. The four of us are members of the House of Lords.

The three men enjoy my company, so I am sure you would hate them all. The weekly card game was held at the Marquis Breckenridge's place in town. Breckenridge folded, and after observing the others were still in, I decided Simon knew something I didn't, so I, too, folded. Eventually the kitty grew rather full. Foxhaven has deep pockets, but Railey doesn't, and for that reason, I began to wonder what the hell the man was doing. In the end, he threw down a letter from Madame Evangeline, for an evening with a lady, as part of his bet."

"He used his liaison as part of his bet?"

"He did, and he lost. To be honest, once I left that night, I didn't think about the game, the evening, or Madame Eve and her damned service again. That is, not until after Wolfe's masquerade ball." The earl twisted the glass of wine in his hand. "The next day, I was invited to the wedding of the marquis. I wasn't actually shocked, since he had been tightly wound like a watch spring for weeks. And a man of his renowned patience like Simon doesn't let anything or anyone rattle him. He can sit through the most heated of arguments in Parliament and never raise his voice, all the while getting his point across. For the last few weeks, he had been biting the head off everyone and picking fights where there weren't any. When a man is as twisted in knots as he was, it's bound to involve a woman."

Miranda grew angrier with every word he uttered. Anger over his neglect to mention the lady he had been with when the wedding proposal had taken place, and that the woman had been she. Yet, when he put two and two together, he would discover she had been the one to hit him that night, and she would have to face the consequences of her actions.

"Please continue."

"Very well. The next morning as...." Andrew paused and stared into the distance.

"As?" she encouraged.

Blinking, he directed his attention back to her. "Nothing important. Anyway, while I searched for something from Simon's desk, at his request, a letter fell out, along with the calling card of Madame Evangeline. I figured Simon no longer needed it and

49

pocketed the card. I had hoped the elusive woman might succeed where I, as of late, had failed. Apparently, even her skills at pairing people can't help me." He turned the bottle upside down, shaking it to get the last drop of red liquid into his glass. "Your turn, my dear."

Miranda thought for a minute about how to phrase her answer, which allowed her anger to spur her on anew. "My aunt paid for this rendezvous."

"Your aunt?"

"Yes. I'd had a miserable evening one night with my all-but-absent betrothed. He treats me like I don't exist, and is happy to ignore me and leave me to grow old in the country."

"Idiot."

"Pardon me?"

Meeting her gaze, he didn't flinch as he answered her question. "I said, he is an idiot. Please continue."

Taking a deep breath, she forged on. "There really isn't much more to tell. My affianced made it clear our wedding was not on his agenda of things to do anytime soon. So, in order to break our contract, my aunt thought it best to lose my maidenhead, thus, he would nullify the agreement."

"I see." What he saw, Miranda wasn't sure, since his expression remained unreadable. The only sign he worked through what she'd told him was the constant rhythm his fingernails made as he tapped them on the table next to him. "Rather an extreme way to get out of marrying someone."

"I suppose you have a better idea?"

"Yes, simply refuse his nonexistent suit."

"If life were only that easy. You see, his estate has been paying for my tutors and my upbringing since my birth. It was an arrangement made between our fathers long ago." She watched Andrew's face for some recognition, for anything that said the words of her story rang a bell of any kind. Nothing—the man appeared to hear the story for the first time.

"So, you fear he will ask for the money back."

"I do, and although my family's estate is in a better place than in the past, it still can't afford to repay all that has been paid out."

"What if I offered to give you the money?"

Picking invisible lint off the cuff of his shirt, he acted as though it was completely normal to offer money to a woman he just met.

She opened her mouth, but no words came forth. His offer took the wind right out of her war-ship's sails. "Why would you do that?"

"Damned if I know." Running a hand through his hair, he looked to the ceiling as if searching for heavenly guidance.

He couldn't really mean to buy her out of her betrothal to himself. And, even if he did, how would she ever pay him back? And why would she trade one shackle to him for a new one? "What would you expect in return?"

"Not your maidenhead, if that is what you are asking. I prefer women who want to be with me for who I am, not for the money I paid out."

Dumbstruck, she sat before him at a complete loss. He offered her money to get out of the contract?

"It's a lot of money."

Rolling his eyes, he shrugged. "I imagine it is."

"What about you? Do you plan to marry?"

"Marry? Are you joking? I can't seem to get a woman to like me for more than a few minutes, let alone agree to swear before God to be my wife for a lifetime."

"What about love?" As soon as the words passed her lips, she wondered why she had blurted them. What did it matter to her, his feeling on love? Yet, there she was, holding her breath, waiting for his reply.

"Having never been on the receiving end of love, I am not sure what it is or if I would recognize it if I found it. Thus, I do not expect it."

The conversation wasn't going as she'd imagined it would. "Surely there are scores of women who would marry you for your money and title."

"Ah, yes, the 'perfectly' boring ones who will do their duty to me and country. Thank you, but no."

"So you aren't betrothed?"

"Not even close."

Red flames burned behind her eyes. He was, in fact, very much betrothed. Grabbing the closest thing, which happened to be her plate of half-eaten food, she flung it at him. It landed nowhere close to its mark.

"What the hell is wrong with you?" He stepped toward the broken china then paused. His gaze moved between her and the pieces on the floor. "I have had enough of this craziness. Good day, lady."

"You son of a donkey's ass."

In the act of opening the door, he paused before slamming it shut again. "What did you say?"

"I said you are a donkey's ass."

"A son of...." He stormed toward her, his boots echoing in the room.

"Well, yes." Concern replaced her anger. In her fit of furious hurt, she had forgotten she was alone in a room with a man she had insulted, and, although she didn't usually hit a person, she had thrown an item or two in the past. Her aunt said it was part of being a redhead. But years of frustration Miranda couldn't voice to the person she most wanted to had resulted in such poor behavior. So, there she was, for a second time, her anger boiling over until she couldn't see past the hurt, and she'd lashed out.

As he stood over her, she scooted back on the

chaise. Andrew's face held an odd mix of confusion and anger. She understood the look, or, at least, the feeling, because she had been feeling similarly about him for weeks. Nay, months, or perhaps years.

He took a deep, calming breath before addressing her. "I have never had that insult hurled at my head before, and now, in the course of a month, I have had it hurled at me with great violence twice." He held his hand inches from her face.

"What are you doing?" she muttered.

Without bothering to respond, he covered her eyes and the bridge of her nose, opening his fingers so he could see her left eye. *Good God, he's mimicking a demi-mask.* After a moment, he pulled the hand away, and her sight returned. However, his face remained close, his anger replaced by brows furrowed in confusion.

"Blessed hell, it's you. The woman from the masquerade!"

She nodded, because there was nothing to say that wouldn't make him sound like a fool. And, in a small sense, the shock on his face played into the guilt she had been carrying for punching him.

"You have a hell of a punch," he said.

"My aunt insisted I learn how to defend myself." Remembering the knuckle pain from hitting him, she rubbed the healed skin.

"I commend her, though I can't quite bring myself to thank her." Andrew sat on the table before Miranda, and she worried for a second it might not hold his weight. He rested his elbows on his knees, his hands clasped tight between them. "I can't remember your full name, Miranda. Would you be so kind as to fill in the gaps? Please, forgive me, I usually am not one to forget a name or a face, but...."

"You usually aren't on the receiving end of a fisticuff?"

A self-deprecating chuckle escaped his lips. "Exactly."

"My name is Miss Beauchamp." She waited to see if the name gave him any pause, but his face remained passive. "Miranda Beauchamp."

Rubbing his upper lip, he asked, "Any relations to the Beauchamps of Windenshire County?"

"Yes. Peter Beauchamp was my father."

"Your lands neighbor mine."

Lands? That's all he considered, after her revelation? Bloody lands? Her inner voice screamed, but she calmly said, "They do, indeed."

Leaning closer, he reached out to touch her but must have thought better of it, as he pulled back at the last moment. "I need you to answer this next question calmly, without violence or anger. Can you do that?"

"I can try." She hated that he thought her a crazy woman, given to fits of hysterics. However, on both occasions, in his presence, she *had* shown him a side even she hadn't thought existed.

"Who is your betrothed?"

Flabbergasted, she could only stare. His face showed nothing but questioning concern, and, for the first time, she realized he knew nothing of her existence. He truly had no idea they were betrothed, that she was his future countess. Miranda wanted to cry. She'd spent her whole life being reared to be his ideal bride. And in most things, she'd succeeded. Yet, unlike what she'd believed in the garden during the duke's ball, it wasn't that Andrew hadn't bothered to learn her name; he genuinely had no idea of the contract between his father and hers. A contract signed days after his birth and years before hers.

"Andrew," she started. His flinch at the use of his given name surprised her. "It's you. You are my betrothed."

"I see." He began to pace, before sitting again, then repeated the action several times. Only his clenched fists remaining at his side showed any sign he had comprehended her words. But, when he opened his mouth to speak, she noticed his hands shook. "I…we…that is, this is the first I have heard of this."

"I believe you." She had no choice but to do so, as the color in his face had drained, leaving him with an unhealthy green tinge; his eyes, always so warm, appearing cold. He was not a man denying her claim, but in shock that she had made it. Empathy filled her, and, if her blasted ankle were not an issue, she would have gone and thrown her arms around him in comfort.

"I do not blame you, now, for punching me, or even throwing a dish at my head. Though I am thankful your aim isn't as good as your fist. If I had been in your shoes, I might have run you down with a carriage."

"The thought did occur to me," she said, in jest, trying to lighten the dark mood because his admission of being ignorant about the contract had done a great deal to mend the pain her soul had suffered with each passing year he hadn't arrived to claim his bride.

He walked to a writing desk at the far end of the room. Sitting down, he opened it, and scratched out a note then, by the sound, she assumed he sanded the ink. Only when she smelled the wax did she know he had sealed the letter with the signet ring on his pinkie. Her mind raced at what and to whom he had written. He stepped outside into the hall and spoke to someone, but, try as she might, Miranda couldn't hear the conversation.

A moment later, he stuck his head in the room again. "Are you comfortable, or do you wish to move to a more private room?"

Surprised by the question and unsure how to answer anyway, she shook her head to show she was not uncomfortable then nodded that she would indeed like to move.

Propping the door open, he headed her way. He leaned down and put one arm under her legs and the other around her waist. "Wrap your arms around my neck, my sweet."

Without thinking, she did as he asked, but protested, "I am too heavy."

"You are quite perfect." He maneuvered through the room, careful not to bump her ankle.

Clutching his shoulder, she found it hard to believe he could lift and carry her weight with so little effort. "What about your coat and my corset?"

"Someone will collect them for us later. For now, the two of us have some serious talking to do."

"Perhaps you can tell me to whom you sent that letter?"

He paused in the entryway, glanced about to ensure no one lingered, then headed up the stairs. On the top landing, he said, "I summoned my solicitor. I am hoping he has the paperwork pertaining to our marriage contract."

"Oh." Miranda couldn't think of anything else to say.

He stared down at her. "I love the delightful way your mouth forms an O."

Nearly doing it again, she stopped and said, "It's rather late in the evening to summon someone, isn't it?"

"It's about ten, I should think, but I pay my solicitors a damned good amount of money to do very little. They had best come when I call."

"Very lordly."

He laid her down in the center of a gigantic bed. "Just efficient."

"Is there not another room for us to wait in?"

'If you are concerned that I plan to breach your virginal barrier tonight, put your mind at ease, I have no such aspirations. But with your ankle, you will be far more comfortable here. There is a private dining room which will allow me to speak to my lawyer and you to remain comfortable."

"I see."

"You sound disappointed."

Was she? Perhaps so. Since the reason to hate him had been taken from her, the charming man she'd kissed had become the man of her dreams once more.

"Perhaps I am."

"Rest assured, once I get to the bottom of this, I hope to make love to you, but it won't be in a strange random room, but in a marriage bed." Heat filled his eyes and laced his words, and then he turned away. "If you plan to break the contract, which I will not contest should you wish to, I will not take from you what is a gift for your future bridegroom."

"Now it is you who sounds disappointed."

"Perhaps I am."

Really? Until he'd answered her in kind, she hadn't been aware she'd spoken aloud.

"Why are you surprised? I made no secret of my attraction to you at the ball. What makes you think it changed simply because you are my betrothed?"

"For one, I punched you in the eye. For another, I have been downright rude to you this evening."

"With good reason, and, if you think those things can delay the amorous appetite of a man, you have a great deal more to learn about my sex than I thought."

"So you believe me about the contract?"

"I believe someone led you to believe, as well as your father, that a union between us is a foregone conclusion. Until I have spoken with the family retainers, I won't have an idea of what has been going on." Andrew peeked out the window to the street below before facing her again. "Either way, I do not doubt your side of the story. You had nothing to gain by telling me, short of the satisfaction of watching all color seep from my face. But, in the end, if you are truly meant to marry me, showing me the extent of your violent nature would be the wrong way to do so."

"I am not violent. You simply bring out the worst in—"

"Shh." He placed a finger on her lips. "I was jesting."

"Oh."

"I warned you about that facial expression."

"You did?"

"Perhaps warned is too strong a word." Before she could reply, he took her lips with his, kissing her deeper and more thoroughly than the first time. Thoughts of who he was didn't stop her, for he remained her betrothed, at least for the moment, so she had every right to kiss and be kissed by him. Perhaps the location wasn't proper, but nothing about their relationship had gone according to plan, so why would this?

One second, she lay on the bed, propped up on pillows, and the next he had her lying across his lap, his arms around her before returning his attention to her with more fervor than the other two embraces combined.

For reasons she didn't understand, he had branded himself on her. Heaven help her, she still wanted Andrew. Not with the schoolgirl crush she'd had as a young teen. The nervousness she'd experienced whenever she'd heard he was at his estate paled in comparison to her present jitters. Small tremors ran through her until they became outright shivers. He responded by tightening his embrace.

How long they sat in each other's arms she wasn't sure, but she became aware of a soft knock on the door leading from the bedchamber to the dining room. Miranda would have giggled at the long-suffering groan Andrew let out if she'd been able to catch her breath.

"Don't you go anywhere," he commanded.

"Where am I likely to hobble to?" The husky tone in her voice surprised her.

"I will be right back. Or at least back as quickly as I can be." He kissed her one last time before striding away far more slowly than usual.

Falling back on the pillows, she smiled. Though her plan for the evening had been to lose her virginity in order to void the betrothal contract, she had no reason to complain. She'd arrived expecting one thing, yet, now, lay there feeling tingly and downright giddy.

She had so many ideas, or perhaps beliefs, about who Andrew, the man, was. And, so far, they'd all been proven wrong. The years Miranda had spent being groomed to be his countess had all been for naught, because the man before her wasn't the man she'd been trained to marry, he wasn't the cold, heartless man she'd believed him to be. No, he was considerate and passionate. Rather than expressing disbelief or anger with her, Andrew had taken the news about their betrothal with concern, and also with anger directed at those who had left him in the dark. She believed he'd been in the dark about the betrothal, just as she believed those who had were about to feel his wrath.

The biggest shock had been the discovery she liked Andrew as a person, as well as an earl. His answer about hiring people to put them to work had been the first of many things to start thawing the ice block around her heart. She had grown up idolizing him, all the while the girls in town would tease her mercilessly about his lack of attention. Yet Miranda had continued to see him through puppy-love eyes, although only as the handsome lord, not the man behind the title. That all changed, however. While none of the people who worked his land ever spoke poorly of him, she'd found fault in him where she could. As the years passed, the faults grew ever larger in line with his neglect of her.

Now, the faults built on misconceptions were replaced with new ideals of a man she might grow to love. Not a young girl's notion of love and marriage to a lord, but one built from the respect of a woman who views life with eyes wide open. Discovering his true wants and needs, she'd concluded they couldn't be satisfied by the porcelain doll she'd been reared to be, but by a partner both in society and, if the kisses he'd graced her with were anything to go by, in the bedroom as well.

Chapter Three

Andrew's attorney stood from the dining table as Andrew entered. "Milord."

"Do not *milord* me," he barked. His anger, growing by the minute, had to be noticeable to Gordon Lynd, of Lynd and Son.

Andrew's missive had been blunt, making his displeasure clear. Not to mention being dragged from Miranda had left him frustrated beyond reason. Leaving her in that bed could very well have been the hardest thing he'd ever done. The same instant attraction he'd felt at the ball, the sizzle between them, hadn't dimmed.

In the instant he'd stepped into the room to find his lawyer drinking the expensive brandy, Andrew had gone from aroused to furious in one step. Sitting in the chair closest to Mr. Lynd, he focused on the servant hovering nearby. The well-trained man fidgeted from one foot to the other. He could not have seemed more uncomfortable if he had walked in on the two men having sex. "You can leave us."

"Thank you, milord." The young man made his escape, leaving Andrew and his solicitor alone.

"You asked me to bring you the betrothal contract." Gordon's voice held no hint he knew Andrew might be close to jumping over the table and throttling him. Instead, the man pulled a leather satchel from the worn saddlebag on the floor by his chair. Untying the leather bindings, he handed over several yellowed pages. "This, as I am sure you aware, was signed on the day you were born. My father is the one who drew up the papers between your father and the late Mr. Beauchamp."

"Actually, I didn't have clue about this contract until about," Andrew glanced at the clock on the mantel, "two hours ago. Shortly before I had you summoned."

Looking at him over the rim of his spectacles, Gordon blinked—repeatedly. "I'm confused."

"*You're* confused?" Jumping to his feet, he ignored the crash his chair made as it hit the wall. "Imagine for a moment my amazement when the lady

I'm spending the evening with informs me she is actually my fiancée."

Horrified, Gordon gaze darted toward the closed door Andrew had entered. "Miss Beauchamp is here—as in the other room?"

"That is none of your business." Righting the chair, Andrew sat again and began to leaf through the pages before him, then gave Gordon a pointed look. "Explain to me why no one has ever mentioned this contract before."

Fear filled the other man's eyes. "I have no idea, milord."

"Not the answer I wanted," Andrew managed through clenched teeth. "What was to happen if I had tried to marry someone else?"

The solicitor pulled another slip of paper from his satchel with shaking hands. "This is from your mother, stating that, on your eighteenth birthday, you were to be told about the contract to prevent you from getting into that very situation."

"And who was to be the bearer of this news?"

Gordon shuffled through other pages. "Since that

would have occurred during my father's time, I am not in possession of that knowledge. I assumed you knew because Mr. Beauchamp said he had been in contact with you, personally, so it made—"

"Mr. Beauchamp? Miranda's father?" He hadn't had contact with any Beauchamp in years, perhaps decades, his recent encounters with Miranda notwithstanding.

"No, sir. Her father passed away when she was but fourteen. This would be her brother. He came in shortly after his father's death to discuss the yearly allowance given to his sister."

"How much have we been giving her?" Not that Andrew cared about the amount, but something smelled like rotten fish.

"Your father willed to her an allowance not to exceed fifty thousand pounds, to be divided annually, with the yearly amount negotiable depending upon the needs at the time. For instance, the year she was to be presented to the regent, additional income could be made available to pay for needed gowns, lodging, maids—you understand. Any moneys left over on the occasion of your wedding would be placed into a trust for any daughters you might have."

It certainly explained why Andrew had never once questioned a large amount of money going to the Beauchamp estate from his own. But he had to figure out what game Miranda's brother played. Working through the papers, Andrew made his decision. He would walk into the other room and declare his hand to Miranda. It would then fall to her to accept his suit or reject it. He hadn't come there to find a bride, but the thought of her turning her back and voiding the contract made him physically ill. Ironic that, before that evening, he would have expected it to be the other way around.

Continuing to scan the papers, he hoped to find anything he might have missed. "You pay her allowance through a lawyer or to Mr. Beauchamp directly?"

"Originally, we paid to an accountant, who then paid for her tutors and living expenses. Upon the death of the father, his son, Daniel, asked for it to go through him, as their accountant was reaching well into his later years. So, for the last, I would say ten years, we have been paying him directly."

"How much was the last amount?" Andrew stared squarely at his lawyer.

"Let me see." Placing a pair of circular spectacles on his bulbous nose, Gordon swallowed hard before running his fingers over the page in the account ledger. "Ah, yes. Over the last five years, we have increased her allowance from one thousand to fifteen-hundred quid. We last increased it four years prior, from seven hundred annually, to one thousand."

"I see."

"Is there anything else I can assist you with this evening? I will, of course, contact Mr. Beauchamp in the morning," Gordon said in a humble voice, busying himself with the buckles on his bag.

"No." Andrew's voice came out harsher than intended, so he placed a smile he didn't feel on his face, forced calm, and lowered his voice. "Make no contact with anyone regarding the matter. I will personally handle this from here."

"Are you certain?"

"Completely. Thank you for coming so quickly. Feel free to order up some food or drink while your horse is brought around."

Excusing himself, Andrew needed to ask Miranda what she knew and determine how much Daniel Beauchamp had thus far filched from his sister. If Gordon was to be believed, and Andrew had no reason to believe him untruthful, then a decade had passed since Daniel and the solicitor had discussed the contract. The notes on the table reflected the same information and more. For the last three or four years, Daniel had managed to convince his lawyers he'd spoken with Andrew and everyone was in agreement to the delay in nuptials. Of course Daniel would delay them, as the moment his sister wed, the money would cease.

But how would Andrew break the news to Miranda that her brother was a snake in the grass?

He opened the door to the bedroom, and Miranda's beauty lit the room, unexpectedly taking his breath away. Sitting in the shimmering candlelight, she resembled a Botticelli goddess. The hem of her skirt had slipped up to her thigh as someone, likely the French maid, had elevated her ankle on no less than three pillows. Miranda smiled at him over the top of a book. Stepping to the side of the bed, he removed the volume from her hands. Careful not to lose her spot, he laid it on the table face down.

"So what did you learn?" she inquired.

"Quite a bit, yet not enough." He sat on the edge of the mattress.

The swelling appeared to be getting worse. In contrast to the bluish ankle, the leg attached to it remained unmarred, shapely and appearing so soft. Temptation rolled through him, and, an hour ago he would have given in, but right then he owed her more. Before his urges overrode his good intentions, he covered her leg down to the calf with a nearby throw."How does your ankle feel?"

"Stiff and throbbing."

"I suspect it will hurt more in the morning. Do you wish me to summon a doctor?"

Shaking her head, she grabbed his hand, but dropped it as if realizing how bold the move was. He gripped her hand and squeezed.

"Will you please tell me what you learned?" she asked.

"We are betrothed. I am indeed your fiancé, and a lousy one at that."

"Please don't be hard on yourself. You didn't know."

How did she manage to be so understanding? He wasn't sure if he could look himself in the mirror again as guilt lit through him like a furnace, so how could she look at him now? "I should have known. Unfortunately, four of the five people involved in the contract able to shed light on why I was kept in the dark are long dead, and their secrets went with them."

"Five?"

"My parents, your parents, and my father's lawyer. Both the lawyer and my parents are deceased."

"As is my father, and my mother ran off to Australia with a soldier half her age. I doubt she will ever come back." Miranda shrugged, but he didn't miss the pain in her eyes.

"So now it's only you, your aunt, and your brother."

Nodding, she smiled. "Sarah is my rock. She took me in long before my mother left. I think my father knew I would be better off with Sarah than in my own home. He wasn't an affectionate man, but he cared for me in his own way."

"And your brother…are you close?"

"No, not really. He never understood why I had to have French tutors and dance lessons, when the family had to sell artwork and furniture. I can't tell you the number of times I tried to get them to use the money for their needs but…." Her voice trailed off.

"Please go on."

"Honest to a fault described my father. Any money given to the family for me because of an understanding—"

"Contract, legal and binding. Sorry, please continue."

"Regardless of the paperwork, if my father gave his word, he never broke it."

The conviction in her words urged Andrew to

77

believe her. Staring at a smudge on his left Hessian boot, he tried to think of how to broach the next topic: her brother. But no matter how many times he practiced the words in his mind, they always seemed harsh and accusing.

Her small, soft hand squeezed and radiated warmth into his. "What is it? I may not know you well." She laughed, and the lyrical sound eased the strain in the room. "I never thought I would say that. I have been trained to know your every want…."

"Are you sure?"

Blank confusion passed over her eyes before his meaning sank in, and she blushed. She intrigued him as her nose turned red and the color spread. "That isn't what I meant."

"I couldn't resist, and now that I have seen you blush, I might have to repeat the process. But you were saying?"

"It seemed like something bothered you is all," she mumbled, pulling out of his grasp to cover her face with her hands.

"Don't hide from me." He pulled them away and

brought them to his lips, placing a single peck into each palm before working small ones along the inside of her wrist.

"I wanted to hate you."

"I understand that." He repeated the caresses on her other wrist.

"I'm very sorry I punched you."

"I'm not."

She pulled her arm back. "You wanted me to punch you?"

He kneeled on the mattress so she had to arch her neck to meet his eyes. "Since it gave me a second chance with my bride-to-be then, for a little pain and some serious jesting at the hands of my friends, I would do it all over again."

"You plan on marrying me?"

He paused. "There is a contract that says we must."

She turned away with an expression of pain. "I never wanted you to feel trapped into marrying me."

Honor played a part in his decision, of course, but, deep down, he feared, if he let her off the hook, she might find someone else.

"Do you feel *trapped*? What I said before still holds; the decision is yours. Would it help if I told you the night at the masquerade I was drawn to you? It didn't matter who you were, I couldn't help but walk across the room to meet you."

"Why?"

"Maybe it was your creamy skin set against the deep red of your dress. Or the sensual curve of your neck. But, to be honest, it was the way you fidgeted from one foot to the other and bit your lip."

His focus settled on her as she bit her lip in response. Groaning, he lowered his head to meet her mouth. She opened on a gasp, and he took the opportunity to deepen the joining. His cock sprang to attention. The minx possessed a power over his libido like no woman ever had.

Her breath came out on a rush of air. "I don't feel trapped."

"I want you to get acquainted with me, the man. Not the earl."

"But they are one and the same." She stared up at

him with wide green eyes.

"No, they aren't. What is my favorite drink?"

"Brandy"

"Food?"

"Potato dishes of any type, but cottage pie is your favorite."

He nodded "My favorite horse?"

"At present, it is a brown stallion with white stockings on three of its hooves. I am unsure of his name."

"Sampson." Andrew smiled. She did know a great deal about him. "Favorite color?"

"Blue."

"You're wrong."

She blinked as if unsure what to say. "But my tutors—"

"Could have no idea that the earl, who, if asked in public, would proclaim his favorite color might indeed be blue, might prefer something else. Yet that the man would in private confess his favorite color to be auburn hair as the firelight reflects in it, making it appear to catch fire. Followed closely by eyes such a deep green, they matched the gown its owner is currently wearing." He waited, let his words sink in, let her see that *the man* was someone only she would know. "So, as you can see, the man is different from his public persona."

"You can't mean that."

"Can't I?"

Miranda appeared to hesitate, as if unsure whether to believe him or not. "None of this makes sense."

"I completely agree with you."

"You do?"

Rolling to his side, Andrew played with the soft curl of hair drooping rather sensually across the swell of her breast. "Why so surprised? Do you think I can make heads or tails of this either? At the masquerade, I had never felt such an attraction. When I walked in here tonight, standing before the parson never crossed my mind. But, now, I can't think of anything else."

"What if we don't suit?"

"We suit."

"You sound so sure, and I hate that I am not. I

am usually so confident, but now I feel lost."

He placed his lips on the base of her neck. "Does this help?"

Extending it, she gave him access to every inch of skin. She offered, he accepted. She smelled like rose hips, her skin the softest he had ever touched. Every inch fascinated him. He had undressed more women than he could count but felt as if she was the first one. Perhaps it was because she belonged to him, or perhaps she was special in a way he had never thought of any other woman. He had no idea how Madame Evangeline had done it, but she'd found the type of woman he desired; one who had been hiding in plain sight.

Chapter Four

Miranda's eyes blurred as his lips touched her bare neck. His hand under her bosom burned, ached in a way she wished would never end, and he wasn't even touching them. Then there were his kisses; the line of light, torturous heat bringing her nerves to a near-breaking point.

She whimpered, exposing more of her neck to him. "Milord."

"Andrew," he whispered against her earlobe. "I do not want to hear 'milord' cross those kissable lips when associated with me, and never when we are in bed."

"But—"

"No buts, and I will include other places where milord is off-limits."

She leaned back, puzzled. His eyes held playful sensuality.

"Oh, I plan to make love to you in every room of every home I own."

She would have gasped, at the very least protested that as a well-bred lady, discussing such inappropriate things should not happen, but his lips caught hers, leaving her unable to remember any protest or what she was protesting in the first place. His tongue coaxed hers into a waltz. Every stroke brought the temperature to furnace levels. Her dress, even with the lacings relaxed, seemed too tight and constricting.

"Shh. Trust me. I can help you." He nibbled her lower lip.

She was unsure what he meant until his hand eased the sleeve of her gown over her shoulder. His touch fueled the flames already licking her skin.

"Too hot," she murmured.

"What's too hot?" His lips made their way down her jawline toward the newly exposed skin, leaving a trail of aftershocks.

"Me—your touch. I can't breathe."

"Relax."

Easy for him to say. She wanted to scream, but instead fell back onto the mass of overstuffed goose-down pillows behind her. With the exception of the thumb on his right hand tracing the underside of her breast, he remained still. As his eyes met hers, the playfulness became a need she didn't quite understand, but imagined, if he felt a small degree of what she did, he might ignite at any moment.

Gazing up at the ceiling, she concentrated on breathing and remembered what a tutor had once told her; when in bed with her earl, Miranda should focus on something—anything—until he'd finished. *Think of the beauty of the countryside, the motherland, or practice the harpsichord in your head.*

"What are you doing?"

She lifted her head. "Thinking of England."

"Really?" he asked, appearing amused by her answer.

Nodding, she returned her attention to the ceiling. "My tutor said that when I was in bed with you, I should look at the ceiling and think of distractions. She must have known the fire would consume me otherwise."

He climbed up over her, obscuring her view of

the red canopy. "You are quite priceless. I think your tutor has offered me a challenge."

"Pardon?" Miranda blinked repeatedly, wishing what he said didn't sound as scary and utterly amazing.

He fondled her left breast and squeezed. "Whatever I do, I want you to turn your attention toward the ceiling."

"And what will you be doing?"

"Everything in my power to make you look away."

"But—"

"Oh, I haven't changed my mind about leaving your maidenhead intact for tonight. I relish the opportunity of claiming that in our marriage bed, but there are other things we can do without taking your virginity."

Her lips formed the O he'd said he liked so much.

"You're looking at me." He pointed up. "I do hope your resolve is stronger than a simple grope of your breast."

"Challenge accepted." Steeling herself with a lung-filling breath, she focused her attention on the center of the canopy where the emerald fabric gathered and began to count the puckers. *One, two, three*—his hand squeezed again. She could have sworn she felt the layers of her skirts rising up her legs but he was obviously trying to get her to break her concentration. She would do no such thing. What number had she been on? Right. *Three. Four, five. Six* was a rather large gather in the canopy fabric. *Seven, eight, nine.*

She hissed as he touched the ties of her pantaloons. Between choppy breaths, she tried to focus. *Nine. No, I already did nine. Ten, eleven*—his hand reached in to caress her most intimate parts.

"Andrew!"

"Ceiling, love. Remember, think about God and country."

"I am quite certain God would consider this a sin."

"God has far more important things to worry about than what you are doing in this bed right now."

He parted her lower lips and a gasp escaped her upper ones. Dear heaven, she finally understood what the maids giggled about. Pleasure filled her, and dampness pooled between her thighs. "You are so wet."

"I'm sorry."

"Sorry? This is the best gift you can give a man. This is proof you enjoy our intimacy. Shows me you are ready to take my—cock deep in your body."

She snuck a peek at him, but he wasn't pay attention to her face. His concentration lay on the area between her legs. "So this feeling deep in my abdomen is normal?"

"Does the feeling make you want more?"

Muscles she had never known she had were coming to life with every touch. "Yes."

"Do you touch yourself, Miranda, when you think you are alone and no one will catch you?"

Somewhere through the fog of passion, she managed one single word. "Where?"

"Where, she asks." He sounded so long-suffering, she giggled. "Here or here?"

His thumb rubbed her in just the right spot as another finger entered her. Unable to form words of any sort, she only shook her head.

"Never? Well, that is something I can't wait to remedy. The thought of you pleasuring yourself makes me want to spill my seed right now."

"You want me to touch myself." Coming up on her elbows, she slammed her knees closed and locked his arm in place. There was no way ever she would touch herself like he was, and certainly not with him watching. Her face burned with mortification as she tried to ease away.

"Relax sweetheart." He kissed the outside of her knee. "And, yes, I most definitely want you to touch yourself."

"Why?"

Resting his cheek against her knee, he grinned. "I want you to be able to tell me everything you enjoy. But how can you tell me if you haven't had the experience? If you have never yourself found out."

"And you want to watch me while I do it…?" she asked, the last part of her sentence so quiet, she wondered if he'd heard.

"Why are you whispering? It's only us." Equally quiet, he answered, "Hell, yes."

"Down there?"

"Right here." Adding some pressure to her clit, he rubbed the sensitive nub until her eyesight blurred and she barely caught the moan that tried to escape. "Maybe here."

"You can't mean you want me to touch…well…inside?"

His gaze met hers, slightly glazed over and filled with a strange hunger. And, if she were the betting sort, she might wager her own were showing a mixture of confusion, shock and embarrassment.

"Why not? It's your body. Who has more right to touch it than you?"

"I didn't think anyone should be touching it. Well, maybe a doctor, if necessary, but he would never look. You look and touch, and I—"

"Do you dislike this?" He moved the digit in and out, each time, the waves of pleasure grew, making her weep.

91

She tried deny it felt good, but she lived by the rule of honestly, so she shook her head.

"Anything I do that you dislike, I need you to tell me. Do you understand? If it hurts, scares you, or if the sensations become too much, I can't know what you are feeling if you don't tell me. Do you understand?"

She nodded and figured what she didn't understand would make more sense later. "What you were doing...is that normal for couples to do?"

"I can't speak for other men, but I quite enjoy touching you, feeling your juices cover my skin, and hearing those lovely little meowing sounds you make like a cat that got the cream."

"Would you wish me to touch you this way, too?"

"Not tonight, but, yes. I am sure I will live in torment until our wedding night, thinking of you running your hands over me—intimately."

She mused at the oddity of them lying on this bed, his hand up her skirts and between her legs. Odd, but not wrong. And more than she'd imagined. Other than Aunt Maggie, everyone had led her to believe, when they were in bed together, the man would stick his *member* in her while she lay quietly and thought of other things. So far, she'd thought of nothing other than what he'd done to her.

"You are very sure we will suit?"

"Have I not convinced you yet?"

She couldn't answer that, nor was she particularly certain he required one from her. As shocked as she had been at his boldness while touching her, his next move left her speechless.

"Look to the ceiling and try and focus."

Managing to count to twenty-three, she thought herself quite improved in her ability to stay on task counting the pleats. That was, until Andrew pulled her knickers clear down to her ankles. He gently stripped them over her sore ankle.

"You are supposed to be concentrating on the ceiling." Although his reprimand sounded stern, it hinted of laughter.

"But you removed my drawers."

"Yes, I did, and, if that shocked you, what I plan

next may send you into a fit of vapors. The ceiling, if you please."

Uncertain didn't begin to describe the feelings coursing through her right then...a sense of adventure, the forbidden, and, she figured, a sense of arousal. Leaning back, she looked at him again but he responded with a raise of a lordly eyebrow. So she was resigned to following his orders.

Until, that was, his tongue lapped between the folds of her most intimate place. She bolted upright and sputtered, unable to utter a single coherent word.

"Be mindful of your ankle."

"My ankle?"

"Yes, this dainty thing connected to an alluring-as-hell leg."

Alluring leg? "You just licked me—down there—and all you can worry about is my blessed ankle?"

"I plan to do it again, too."

"But why would you want to? People don't do that, do they? That can't be permitted; it's not right. You can't possible enjoy...that."

He appeared quite put out, lying between her legs, resting his chin on his fist. "Which of those questions would you like me to answer first?" Not waiting for her to respond, he said, "I need for you to listen because this is very important. When we are married, we can do anything we want in our bed. Providing it's together and, above all, consensual. Do you understand?"

She nodded because what should she to say to that? He seemed quite certain it was permissible, and, as she assumed he had more experience in such matters, she couldn't argue without facts. She would have to ask Aunt Sarah in the morning. But, somehow, asking her aunt seemed a little too wicked, even for Sarah.

"Next, although I can't speak for others, as I don't discuss my sexual appetite, I am certain that the men of my acquaintance do this, if not regularly, on occasion."

"No!"

"Yes!"

"Not the marquis or the duke. Not men of

such...."

"Yes, them, especially them. Now, your last two questions can be answered together. I very much would like to do this to you. I want to hear you moan with pleasure, taste your arousal, and feel your orgasm. If you would only lie back again and let me have my wicked way with you the only way I can tonight."

"But...."

"Trust me, when I am done with you, there will be no doubt how well we will suit."

Though still uncertain, she did as she was told and kept her eyes open. His hands wrapped under her thighs and eased them apart. Uncertain what to do, she intertwined her fingers on her tummy and squeezed.

The first breath of air touched her like the hint of a summer breeze, warm and hinting at rain to come. He kissed her inner thigh, and it took everything she possessed not to jump. The tiny kisses he'd made on her shoulder and neck, that she had so loved earlier, trailed to her apex. He gripped her legs and blew again. Her legs shook, whether from her desire or expectation, or perhaps fear of the unknown, she was unsure.

As he ran his tongue along the sensitive nub he had rubbed earlier, the initial shock wore off and warmth filled her. The shaking increased, but now she understood, and she wanted more. She was unable to control her moan, and he chuckled, a low male, satisfied laugh that vibrated against her and took her breath away. He circled and added pressure with his tongue. When he dove inside her, she lifted her hips, wanting him deeper within her. Her fingers wrapped into his soft hair, pressing him against her, demanding more, desperate for him to make good on his promise.

"God, yes," he murmured, as if her response spurred him on. Testing it, she repeated the process and was rewarded with a moan from him.

His ministrations increased until stars formed before her eyes. The muscles deep in her abdomen tightened, tension built within her, and she tried to pull away, but placing a hand on her belly, he held her still. Suddenly weightless, she would have floated

97

to the ceiling if not for the firm hold he had on her, or perhaps the death grip she had on the bed. Then her limbs seized, her eyelids lowered, and she began to tremble. Only as the tremors eased and she returned to a more natural state did he pull away. He stroked her thighs, helping to calm her before easing her dress down her legs.

When she opened her eyes, he lay beside her, staring at her with an odd light in his eyes. "So, will we suit?"

Unable to face him, she draped an arm over her face and said, "Holy hell, we will suit."

Chapter Five

Andrew stood in the entry hall of Miranda's aunt's townhome. Though it was not in the fashionable part of London, no one would think less of the living quarters where she resided. Yet, to say her Aunt Sarah had been put out by his appearance would have been an understatement. He, of course, still needed to put together who had knowledge about the betrothal agreement. He damned well needed to get to the bottom of what was going on. Heads would be rolling.

Not that it mattered. The evening before had proven to both he and Miranda that marriage would be the most prudent course of action.

For the first time in his life, he understood chivalry. He might have had a full-blown cockstand for much of the night, but he had done nothing about it. As his future countess slept the sleep of the sated, he'd laid next to her, watching and marveling at the turn his life had taken in a few short hours. He had instructed that his carriage, empty at the time, sit in front of her house early in the morning, then be taken away shortly afterward—a ruse to make any early bird believe he had simply come calling and taken Miranda for a ride, once a believable amount of time had passed.

He and Miranda had then arrived at her home at a decent hour that would make any neighbors believe she had left for a morning stroll with a suitor. Returning to her steps in the arms of her betrothed might have raised an eyebrow, or, in the case of Sarah, two, but it couldn't be helped. There was no way she could maneuver the steps on her own.

Left to cool his heels in the front hall since arriving over a half hour earlier, he wondered how long Sarah would allow her spite to overrule her good breeding, and how much his virginal lady had told her.

"Madame will see you now," the liveried footman announced, waving toward the stairs and up to the first floor of the house. "Second room on the right."

"Thank you." Andrew climbed the dark, wood-paneled staircase to the sitting room. Tapping lightly, he waited only a second before opening the door.

Sarah glared, but, too well-bred to do more than that, she curtsied prettily before bowing her head. "Milord."

"Madame." He nodded his head before turning his attention to Miranda, currently ensconced on a chaise lounge in the corner by the window, with her elevated ankle under a blanket. He winked, reveling in the blush that quickly covered her cheeks. "Miranda."

"Andrew," she whispered, a secretive smile forming on her lips.

"Milord, please be seated." Sarah indicated the chair next to Miranda. "I have ordered some tea."

"Thank you, tea is much appreciated." Feeling he had given her the respect due, he turned his attention to Miranda. "How is your ankle, my dear?"

"Much better, milor…Andrew. Thank you for inquiring."

Clearing her throat, Sarah commanded his

attention. Once she had grown past her dislike of him, he thought they may become great friends. He liked her already. "My niece filled me in on a few items. She tells me though you tended to her injury all evening, you didn't take her maidenhead."

"Sarah!" Miranda sat straight, disrupting the pillows around her on the chaise.

Andrew raised his hand to calm her, picking up one frilly lace pillow, which had fallen to the floor. As she was literally surrounded by pillows he had no idea where to place it and finally gave up, placing it on the window seat behind him. "She is correct. I didn't take advantage of the situation," he replied. *Even though I wanted to.*

Sarah nodded with approval. "She also informs me you were not aware of the betrothal agreement."

"I was not."

She leveled her keen brown gaze on him. "How can this be so?"

"I wish I knew, exactly—"

Sarah interrupted, thumping the carpeted floor with the cane he hadn't been aware she held. He doubted she needed the thing for the purpose of walking, but more for effect. "This is not to be taken lightly. You must investigate how this lack of knowledge happened."

"I have already put my solicitors on it, but would request your help in the matter. It would appear Miranda's brother is well aware of the agreement and has, over the last few years, increased the amount of the allowance required to maintain Miranda's standard of living."

"Bollocks! The amount given to me to pay her bills has decreased."

"I assumed as much," Andrew replied drily. Another nail in the already nearly sealed coffin against Miranda's brother. Exhaling forcefully, he rubbed the tension from between his eyes. Lack of sleep, anger, and unsated sexual needs did not a clear mind make. "What can I do to help you?"

"I ask you to call for her brother. I doubt if I do so he will come, but if you were to say his poor sister has decided to marry someone else…."

Andrew rose and strode to the window behind

him, staring out at the busy street below before turning back to look at Sarah.

"That might get him here rather quickly."

"You intend to marry my niece?"

His eyes never wavered from hers. "I am most earnest."

"And you, Miranda…you still wish to become his countess?"

"More than anything in the world."

Sarah nodded, walked to the pull cord, without the use of the cane, and pulled once for a servant. "Very well. I want nothing more than to see Miranda happy, and, somehow, you have convinced her you are the man to do it. And the gentleman I see standing before me does indeed seem to be up for the job."

She wrote out a letter then sanded and sealed it before giving it to the footman. "See this placed in Daniel's hands by nightfall. You can return with him on the morrow, though I suspect he will be leaving on horseback first thing in the morning."

Miranda shifted on the chaise. "Your plans, milord?"

"I have sent one of my men to the church at Windenshire. He has a letter for the chaplain with directions to begin the reading of the banns on Sunday. As today is Thursday, there is no reason to believe Daniel will be there to hear them."

"I can't believe Daniel would steal from you," she said in a small, broken voice. Her fingers fidgeted with the lace on one of the pillows.

"We haven't discovered where the money went. If he has used it to make much-needed repairs, or to better the lives of your servants, I have no reason to care that he used the resources. If they were for more selfish reasons, I will be less able to look away." Andrew crouched before her and grasped her hands in his. "He has taken a great deal of money from you. Not me. And he has created a situation where I might unwittingly have married another."

"But he is my brother."

"That is the only reason I am not on my way up there to smash his face with great force." Unable to stand the sadness on her face, Andrew leaned forward and kissed her temple. "I promise to take into account your love for your sibling, no matter how misplaced it might be."

"Promise?" Her misty eyes met Andrew's.

"Promise. I just don't have to like him."

"Fair enough."

The smile, though tentative, told him she trusted him to take care of the situation with care. Her happiness had suddenly became very much intertwined with his. Wolfe had told him when he'd met his fiancée, Wolfe had said almost immediately no other woman would compare. Yet, for Andrew and Miranda, it hadn't been so simple. He had nearly walked out a couple of times, Miranda's intense hostility and hate toward him palpable. After the incident in the maze, he never would have given her a second chance for a 1Night Stand liaison, had he known it was her. But once he had known the reason behind her feelings, he'd understood completely. She'd had years to build hostility and discontent with him, while he'd had less than twenty-four hours to reconcile his conflicted feelings of a beautiful masked lady with amazing boxing abilities. But it bothered him he could have lost her without knowing she had been his to lose.

The door clicked softly and Sarah left them alone. Andrew gazed into Miranda's eyes, only to have her throw herself at him and kiss him. Although taken by surprise, he caught her easily and, ensuring the care of her ankle, he pulled her tight.

His little virgin vixen had a hidden fire he planned to stoke at every opportunity. Maneuvering to sit on the chaise beside her, he allowed her the lead on the kiss until her hand trailed down his back, and over his hips to his thighs.

Pulling away, he stayed her touch. "I can't take much more."

"I simply want to touch you the way you have touched me."

"And I promise you may touch me anywhere your heart desires, once we are wed."

"Is a special license an option?" she asked, biting her plump lower lip, leaving him breathing hard. Damn, if she brought him low already, as a virgin with no experience, what would she do when he awakened her sexual side to its full potential?

He stood, praying desperately for strength. "You said in the carriage just this morning that, should we marry, you wanted it to take place in the church on my lands, before your friends and those who have been less than kind to you through the years. Though I personally would have told them to take a jump in the nearest river."

"Yes, but they never believed I was promised to you. I want them to see us wed so they—"

"Can eat crow? That I do understand."

"Is that petty?"

"I think it's human nature."

She reached forward and rested a warm palm on his upper thigh. "Four weeks seems a very long time."

"Right now, it seems like an eternity," he said between gritted teeth.

"Let me touch you. It's terribly unfair that I feel so unprepared for our wedding night. You are so much more experienced in giving pleasure, as you demonstrating amply well last night. I know next to nothing."

"That is the way it's supposed to be for well-bred ladies."

"It doesn't have to be." Her fingers worked closer to the growing bulge in his pants. Images of her wrapping the, dainty digits around his hard cock dropped the last bit of argument he had formed. He gripped her wrist, and a whimper of protest escaped her lips. She evidently believed he would prevent her exploration. But he placed her hand over the prominent bulge and she gasped.

"It's so—hard." She traced the outline of it through his britches. "Is it always like this?"

"Around you, yes."

"What about when you aren't around me?"

Could he remember that time less than twenty-four hours ago? "Then it is soft and slightly smaller."

"It grows then?"

"For you, yes."

"Take it out so I can see it."

"It is called a cock, and, no, your aunt might be back any moment."

Apparently not listening to a word he'd said, she worked the buttons of his pants. "She shan't come in, that I can promise."

He went to argue, but she slipped a hand inside and wrapped it around him. All coherency fled. The soft palm added just enough friction and, when she squeezed, small beads of sweat broke over his forehead. His balls tightened with the need for release. Finally, he had to lock his knees to prevent them from knocking.

"Like velvet," she murmured. "I hadn't expected that."

Clenching his jaws, he managed, "What, dare I ask, did you expect?"

"I expected something sharp that would cut my maidenhead." She grinned up at him then faltered. "You don't seem to be enjoying this. When you touched me, I enjoyed it very much. What am I doing wrong?"

Taking a deep breath, he forced himself to relax, all the while delaying his release. Releasing a clenched fist, he caressed her cheek. "You are doing everything right. I am fighting my need to make love to you. In doing so, it may appear I am in pain."

"Oh." Satisfied, she went back to what she had been doing.

He, meanwhile, died a slow, excruciating death with every stroke, payment for every sin he had ever committed through his life coming due. Nerves nearly snapped, and the natural instinct to wrench up her skirts and dive into her nearly undid him. Instead, he held onto his baser instincts by the finest of threads. She wanted to explore his body, eager to see what the male anatomy looked like. And, if this allowed for an easier, less frightening wedding night, then it would be worth it. Or so he kept repeating to himself.

Think of England.

Not helping.

Think of crops and rotations.

Not that either.

Think of—

Her tongue touched the tip of his cock.

Fucking hell!

"What are you doing?" he croaked.

"I wanted to taste you." She licked her lips like the cat that got the cream.

"Why?"

She pouted, and he wanted to take that bottom lip into his mouth and suck on it. "Because you did something similar to me; it seemed only reasonable that I would do it to you."

"Your thought process might be the death of me."

"But it is done, is it not?"

"Oh, it's done."

"Good."

The joy in her voice, as well as the enthusiasm, forced him to change his tactics. He'd gone about things all wrong. If he wanted her to learn about him then showing her what pleased him made a hell of a lot more sense. Everything she did, he wanted more of. Closing his eyes, he fought the need to grab her hair and push his cock deep into her throat.

Instead, he lifted his arms and gripped behind his neck. Intertwining his fingers, he held strong where he stood. She licked and sucked and explored the slit

112

where his seed seeped out. Finally, she took him between her lips and deep into her mouth.

Fireworks exploded behind his closed eyelids, and he threw his head back with a load groan. "Hell!"

Only when his balls tightened did he step back, yanking his pants up. Looking at Miranda nearly completed his undoing.

Beaming up at him, she said, "That was quite nice."

"Nice?" She'd nearly brought him to his knees, and she called it *nice*?

"I would like to do that again."

"So would I."

"Honestly?" Her face lit up like an eighteen-candle candelabra.

Leaning in, he kissed her. Words couldn't express what he wanted to convey, and a sudden fear consumed him that those feelings might be akin to love.

Chapter Six

Miranda had ceased listening to her brother twenty minutes earlier. After dragging her out of her bed, he'd thrown her dressing gown at her and demanded she meet him in the library downstairs. Although her ankle might not have been as swollen as before, the ugly purple and blue bruises showed it hadn't yet healed. She had hated to call the footman from his rest, but as he arrived dressed and by her bed within moments, it seemed a good guess all the servants were up.

Daniel said nothing as they helped her into the room with the aid of two more footmen. Unlike her husband-to-be, who had easily lifted her weight, the poor footmen, being much smaller in stature, hadn't even attempted to carry her, but offered her their shoulders. When she finally settled, a maid placed a shawl over her lap for modesty and the servants all vacated the room. Leaving her the soul focus of her brother's wrath.

"How did you get here so fast?" she finally broke from her musings to ask. But once the words had slipped past her lips, she remembered she wasn't supposed to know he would be arriving.

His look told her he thought she might be addled. "Did you expect me to simply allow you to marry a man when you were contractually bound to another?"

"You make me sound like a piece of chattel," she mumbled, though not loud enough for anyone to hear. She wondered when her brother had become so pompous. They hadn't been close, but she had rather liked him before this.

"Do you love this new man?"

Did she love him? She wasn't sure. She had been so infatuated with being his countess and, like most girls in the village, she'd had a teenage crush on him. The only difference being she'd genuinely believed she would be his countess one day, while the others could only dream.

"I supposed I might be or, at least, could be one day."

Could she love Andrew? If the man Andrew

appeared to be turned out to be the man she'd spent the last two days with, falling in love with him would be little hardship. He appeared to treat those dependent on him with dignity. None of her tutors had spoken ill of him. Other ladies swooned when he walked into a room, or so Miranda had been informed. But, in truth, his assertion that, although he wanted to marry her, the decision was hers to make, proved the merit of the man.

The waiting silence from her brother alerted her she had missed something important. He stood over her, hands on hips. "Well, what do you have to say?"

She couldn't very well admit she had not been paying attention without receiving another earful, so she improvised. "I didn't think you actually cared what I had to say."

Where the hell was Sarah? She should have been there with her. Sarah hadn't gone out that evening, and it had been her and Andrew's crazy plan to bring her brother there anyway. Andrew and Sarah had established quite a friendship over dinner that evening. He had left briefly to *freshen up* and *deal with a few things*, but had returned shortly before afternoon tea. Neither Miranda or Andrew had been left alone again by her Aunt Sarah, which may have had something to do with the conversation Miranda started once Andrew left—wanting to learn all there was about sex. Sarah, never one to balk, explained a great deal more than Miranda had expected and nothing like her tutors had.

"Enjoy yourself, gel. None of this *lie there and let him take his pleasure* nonsense. If you want something, you tell him, or, better yet, show him what you want. But, I have a feeling your Andrew will take great care to make sure you enjoy it, too."

From there, Miranda worked up the nerve to ask a great many things. She didn't wish to be ignorant on her wedding night. Sarah brought books from her personal library to aid in the education of Miranda. Ensconced safely in her bedroom, she'd opened the first book only to slam it shut again. Though she had thought she was alone, she'd nevertheless checked to be sure that was still the case. Naughty and exciting were equal emotions flaring within her.

The sounds of finger-snapping beside her ear drew her attention. "Miranda, would you listen to me, please? This is damned important, and your daydreaming is not helping the matter."

"As it happens, I was in the middle of actually dreaming when you dragged me from my bed, Daniel. That I am unable to focus lies on your shoulders." So she lied. Thinking about doing some of the things in that book with Andrew had her unable to pay attention, but Daniel didn't need to know that. "Besides, this can wait 'til morning."

"I will get your agreement to call it off whatever agreement you have with this new man, or you shall not sleep at all."

"Why are you so worried about this? The man in question has agreed to pay off any amount we would owe the earl." *Consider that for a moment, dear Brother.*

"We have a contract."

"Yes, you do," the familiar, sensual voice of Andrew said. He stood with his shoulder pressed against the door frame. *How long has he been there?*

"Of course, it wouldn't matter if the earl in question had no idea he was betrothed, now, would it?"

Daniel's eyes got so wide, Miranda feared they might pop from their sockets and roll across the floor. "Lord Windenshire."

Ignoring Daniel, Andrew picked up a pillow from one of the chairs, dragged a foot stool over, placed the pillow on top, then lifted her ankle to elevate it. "How is this feeling?"

"It throbs."

"How in heavens did you get down here?" His concern warmed her.

"Two footmen assisted me."

"You should have remained up in bed, resting." He placed a kiss on her forehead.

"What happened to your ankle, Miranda?" Daniel asked, if only just taking in the state of things.

"She was involved in a carriage accident and lucky this is the only injury she sustained. I am surprised that you are only now getting around to asking about it."

No one but Aunt Sarah had ever stood up for her.

Andrew gave her a wink before turning back to her idiot brother. "So, when were you planning on telling me about the contract, Daniel? Perhaps a better question would be, when did you realize that if you never let me in on the secret, the money would keep rolling in?"

"Our father informed me shortly before he died that I needed to contact you when Miranda came of age to make sure you presented her to the Regent for her coming out. When I came to town to do that, your lawyers informed me your mother wished for you not to be told until such a time as you were ready to wed. Or when you reached twenty-one."

A chill ran down her spine as she watched Andrew clench a fist. "So you saw the golden opportunity and couldn't pass it up."

"The estate needed a large and immediate influx of cash. Miranda had all the dresses she needed, yet I was unable to keep servants employed or the roof from rotting over my damned head," the ever-indignant Daniel dared to announce, his chin held high. Miranda feared he might find a set of knuckles making contact with that very chin any moment.

"I would have given you the money," Miranda said in hope of easing some of the hostility.

"As would I," Andrew agreed.

She observed his proud face, and her heart filled. He would have given her brother money, and she believed him as much as she knew the sun would rise in a few hours. She wanted to reach up and kiss him, tell him how much that meant to her, but knew the opportunity would come later.

"How could I have been sure? And if you think I spent a penny of that money on myself, I didn't. It went to crops and improvements. Father didn't understand the first thing about money or running an estate, which is why everything needed attention."

Some of the tension left Andrew's shoulders, enough she no longer feared he would punch Daniel. But, just in case, she took his hand in hers and urged him to sit next to her. That he did so showed the power she wielded. She needn't fear he wouldn't respect her wishes.

"So this other suitor story was just a ruse to get

me here?"

"As it happens, Miranda and I met by chance last evening. She knew who I was, but for reasons we all know, I had no earthly clue who she was. That being rectified, I have every intention of marrying your sister. Not because of a stupid agreement on a piece paper between two old men but because I seem to see what no one else has; the genuine, amazing beauty of this woman, both inside and out."

Aunt Sarah cleared her throat.

"Of course, Sarah knew her worth as well," he added. "Which is why I hope she will spend a great deal of time with us. But this is what I want you to hear, Daniel; it is completely within Miranda's right to reject my suit."

"She wouldn't dare." Daniel took a menacing step toward her.

Standing, Andrew made a move toward her brother, but stopped at Miranda's touch. "It is completely within her right to reject my suit." He enunciated each word clearly. "Do I make myself clear?"

Daniel stumbled into the nearest chair. "Yes, milord."

"If that should happen, which I hope it does not, Miranda will keep the monthly allowance my father left for her. She will owe me not one penny. You, on the other hand, will owe your sister every cent you took from her, because it was her money to use, not yours. If she decides to forgive the grievance you've committed, that it her choice, as it has nothing to do with me."

Sarah spoke then. "I believe my niece has quite a lot to think about. It's late, Daniel, and I have a bed made up for you so you won't have to awaken a household ill-prepared for your late appearance. When it's a decent hour, I will have a footman take a message informing your staff that you are here."

Miranda bit her lip to prevent her saying something that would get her into more trouble with her brother, like yelling *hurrah* at her aunt's comeuppance of her brother. He might have come in thinking he had the upper hand, but it had become quite evident he walked on thin ice.

"Perhaps, since he awakened your household." Andrew looked Daniel square in the eye, as if daring him to counter his commands, "A maid or two from his house can be sent over to assist in the packing for Miranda? And you, Sarah, of course."

Wondering if she had somehow missed the part of the conversation where anyone had announced they were traveling anywhere, Miranda braced herself and asked, "And where are we going?"

"I talked with the Duke of Foxhaven this evening." He looked at her in surprise, as if thinking she should know his every move. Then grinned at both her and her aunt. "He would be honored to have you both stay with him until his wedding at the ducal estates."

"We have invitations to the duke's nuptials." Sarah, rarely impressed with anything, actually appeared to fight the need to squeal in glee. Invitations to the year's most-talked-about wedding was one thing. Being asked to stay at the ducal estates would be a true feather in her aunt's turban.

Andrew looked at Sarah as if she were daft. "But

of course." He turned back to Miranda "I thought from there, we will travel to Windenshire and you can start planning for the wedding, if that is what you choose. There are three modistes willing to start on your gown tomorrow. You have your choice of which one."

"So, in one breath, you have said I may still choose, yet there are three woman I must choose from to get my gown started tomorrow. Is it really still my choice?" Miranda rose what she hoped was a haughty eyebrow.

"It still is, up until the moment we say I do." He lowered his voice making the comment more intimate and just for her ears. She could only stare up at him unable to make any word form let alone pass her lips.

"Daniel, you may stay in the room at the end of this hall. I am taking to my bed. Andrew, if you would be so kind as to make sure Miranda is comfortable and secure in her bed. I assume I will see everyone for breakfast. I will have the table set for four." Sarah waved them off with a yawn.

Andrew didn't wait for Daniel to leave before

lifting Miranda into his arms and asking her the direction to her room. He took the stairs with no effort, as though she weighed nothing. After helping her into bed, he hung her dressing gown on the hook by her changing screen, before proceeding to take off his overcoat. She had failed to notice earlier he hadn't been wearing a vest or a jabot. For him to have run out of his residence without being immaculately dressed meant he had rushed to her side and let nothing delay him. Bare-chested, wearing only pants, he leaned over to blow out the single candle.

She finally got her head and mouth to work together. "What are you doing?"

"Making sure you are *comfortable and secure.* Just following Aunt Sarah's orders."

"I don't think she meant for you to sleep here." Lifting the blanket to her chin, she knew the action was silly even as she did it, but, somehow, last night, when they had been in a strange bed in a strange room, it had been different than being in her bedroom under her aunt's roof.

"Oh, I am quite certain she did. Besides, people

will talk if they see me leaving your house now. They will think Sarah and I are meeting, and we can't have that."

"And I suppose no one will have noticed you storming into the house."

"I didn't storm." He folded the covers down and arranged a pillow under her ankle, before starting to slip in beside her.

"You sure about that?" How she wished he hadn't blown out the candle so she could see his face.

He paused, one leg in the bed. Then he laughed, climbing all the way in. "I might have stormed a little. I find I am quite protective where you are concerned."

Miranda turned on to her side, feeling warmed by his words, and smiled into the darkness. Andrew pressed against her, one hand coming to rest on her breast. She didn't argue or complain, only took a deep breath and snuggled into him more. "You sure the duke doesn't mind us intruding on his day?"

"Nonsense. There will be hundreds there, and he offered a room. You will like his duchess." Andrew's voice started to fade off with a yawn. "Besides, being newly in love himself, he believes everyone should be."

"And are you? In love?" she whispered, uncertain if she wanted the answer.

A long silence fell over the room, and she feared he might not answer. But, eventually, in a hushed voice, he said, "I believe I might be."

Chapter Seven

Four weeks never passed so fast. The morning after Andrew confronted Daniel, the announcement appeared in the morning paper. Banns were read at the local parish near their homes the following Sunday. The footman sent to deliver the news to the parson stayed to gauge the reaction of the same girls who had taunted Miranda in town, and those who had believed the earl would never make good on his contract to marry Miranda had returned with news of their shock, and the delight of the townsfolk of the upcoming nuptials. Miranda had been overjoyed and somewhat ashamed that she cared what the other girls thought.

"I promise, everyone will believe this is a love match," Andrew had told her.

The simplest touch of her hand on his cheek made it impossible to stand from the breakfast table that morning. His cock was harder then he remembered it ever being. Of course, he couldn't remember his lust being unfulfilled in years either. Now he stood before the parson with Andrew's three closest friends by his side. The new Duchess of Foxhaven had insisted she and the duke should delay their honeymoon until after Andrew's wedding, and the duke, completely infatuated with his wife, did nothing but acquiesce to her wishes.

Andrew couldn't believe the change his life had taken—all the result of a punch to the nose. Miranda took his breath away in a pale cream gown, her hair like a fiery halo, pinned up in a Grecian coif with tendrils framing her face. She'd broken with tradition and asked her aunt to walk her down the aisle.

"You came." His voice seemed huskier than normal. Although he'd believed she would, a small part of him—the part that felt guilty for the pain she had been through—had worried she would give him what he believed he deserved and stand him up at the altar. Relief flooded through him, allowing his shoulders to relax as a weight lifted.

"I did."

She glowed with an inner beauty that blinded

him. Joining hands, they faced the minister, whose lordly voice rang out to the standing-room-only wedding in his church. Andrew should have listened more closely to what the man had to say. But, in truth, his entire focus stayed directed on Miranda.

Since the announcement in the paper, he had been the ultimate gentlemen, escorting her and Sarah wherever they wished to go. He attended every ball Miranda received an invitation to. Her joy in being invited overruled his desires not to go. And the hostesses invited her to every single blasted ball held, as were the other *House of Lords* wives. The ton clambered to meet the new wives and claim an association.

He hadn't known true frustration until two weeks earlier, when Miranda's well-mended ankle finally allowed her to dance. He'd gritted his teeth when men, eager to fill her dance card, swarmed and demanded her attention.

"The waltzes are mine," he had said in a loud tone, daring any of the young whelps to test his stake. And Miranda had danced beautifully, never missing a step, and after each waltz, it required every bit of his self-control not to throw her over his shoulder and find a private room in which to claim her innocence.

After one particular dance, he'd found needs so blatantly obvious, she'd had to walk him off the dance floor and guide him to the well-lit garden patio. His hand had clutched the stone railing until the rock cut into his palms.

"Why are you waiting?" she asked. "I am yours for the taking, if you will but have me."

"You have waited twenty-plus years for me. The least I can do is wait a few more weeks for you."

She grazed his cheek with her lips, bestowing the softest and most chaste of kisses. "You are very sweet, but you hide it well."

"Let's keep that between us, shall we?"

Taking in the beauty of his bride, he let his joy show. It was considered bad ton to wear one's heart on his sleeve, but Andrew had never particularly cared what was considered socially acceptable or not. He wanted the room to accept the contract meant nothing, but his heart wanted, needed, to have the woman beside him for the rest of his life.

"I will."

As they walked in the open air, he handed Miranda a bag of coins to distribute to the children who had come out to witness their lord wed. She would be a good countess to them, making sure the families who worked his land were taken care of. She had proven such that very week when she'd brought baskets of food to two families in need, one a widow whose husband had died, and the other had welcomed a new mouth to feed.

Once back at the estate, with the guests fed, cake cut, and rounds made, Miranda leaned in to whisper in Andrew's ear, "How much longer must we stay?"

Concern filling him, he touched the back of his hand to her forehead. "Why? Are you feeling all right?"

"I am ready to become your lawful wife in every way God intended. I do not wish to wait any longer."

Andrew couldn't breathe. A month of frustration and vivid, erotic dreams blended with hours of awake fantasies had made it impossible to get any work done. He'd been useless at Parliament, and, if not for his steward, his lands would be in worse shape than his nerves. Yet, his vixen of a wife stood before him, batting her eyes like a harlot in the body of a virgin goddess.

The shock on Andrew's face forced Miranda to bite her lip to prevent a chuckle. The poor man had been torturing both of them without good reason. She wanted him to have his moment of chivalry, but only frustration could describe the feeling he caused. She wanted him to touch her, kiss more than her lips. She wanted his hands on her body, on her over-sensitive skin.

Once he pulled himself together, he asked, "What the hell kind of virgin are you?"

"The kind that is sick to death of being a virgin. So, do you intend to take care of this issue or not?"

Grabbing her hand, he pulled her behind him. "Ever your servant." He approached his butler, who stood in the corner of the ballroom. The reddish tinge on the normally stoic man's face revealed he knew exactly what his master had planned. With a bow, he wished them a good evening.

"Evening?" Miranda arched an eyebrow at her new husband.

"Oh, more likely a few days."

"You can't be serious."

Stopping, he lifted her into his arms and took her into the private chambers of the earl and countess, a section of the house she had yet to visit.

Addressing the footman, he said, "No one is to disturb us. No one. Any food may be left by the door to the lord's suite, and I will get it."

"Yes, milord."

Once inside the chamber, Andrew placed her on her feet, then began to work at the tie around his neck while leading her to a large room in the back covered in gold trim and ornate carvings. He was out of his overcoat, vest, and shirt before she had taken in half the room.

"You can explore the room to your heart's content later. Allow me to play ladies maid and help you out of your gown."

"It's amazing."

"The gown or the room?"

"Both, but I meant the room."

His fingers were like whispers against the bare skin exposed on her back. "How do I get these things undone?"

"The lacings are inside at the bottom."

"It's beautiful but it needs to come off," he said, easing the dress from her. Grasping her shoulders, he pivoted her to face him, then gulped. "Good God in heaven."

The modiste had created her chemise and petticoat of the sheerest silk material, and the corset, which usually covered at least the bottom half of her breasts, lay beneath, leaving a clear view of her nipples under the chemise. And it had been her decision to go without pantaloons.

Recovering from his shock, he reached for her. His lips were hungry for hers, his fingers working her nipples into hard, aching nubs. She wanted more. And the friction of the fabric against her skin only made the ache grow.

She moaned and rested her hands on his bare arms. "Get this corset off me."

"Can you breathe with it on?"

"Well, yes, but—"

"Then it stays, you minx. I want to make love to you in this."

"But we have to be naked. All the books show people naked."

Drawing back, he searched her face. "What books?"

"The books Aunt Sarah lent me."

Breathing hard, he raised his eyes toward the ceiling and cupped her breasts with his hands. "You are very dangerous."

"I simply wanted to be more active in our lovemaking."

"If you are any more active, I might never survive to take your maidenhead."

"We can't have that." Lowering her hands, she stood stiffly and faced forward like one of his footmen. "Will this help?"

"You. Are. A. Minx."

She stole a peek at her husband and said, "You've said that already."

"If you have no care for your safety, I will have to take it in hand."

"Please do." She never imagined that lovemaking could be so playful. One second, her feet were firmly on the expensive silk carpet, the next she lay flat on her back on the plush bed.

"Don't move."

By the sound of his voice, she didn't venture to shift an inch.

Other than a stout curse as his foot hit the bedpost, the only sound she heard was the remainder of his clothing hitting the floor. And, finally, the bed lowered from his weight as he climbed over her. He pulled her petticoat up over her thighs and gathered it at her hips until his hands found her apex. Spreading her folds, he eased a finger inside. Throwing her head back, she groaned. His touch soothed the fire deep within, not putting it out, but tapering it so it didn't consume her.

"You are so wet."

"I have been wet for hours." She lifted her head to kiss his lips.

The thin hold on his self-control broke and he returned the kiss feverishly, his fingers working her into the same passion he had aroused in her before. She should tell him to slow down, but worried if he didn't claim her, she would burst into flames. Sliding her palms over his chest, she moved them up to his shoulders and pulled him closer. She ached to get closer.

"You have to slow down," he mumbled against her lips. "Trust me on this, please."

"I can't stop." She whimpered, needing him more than the air she breathed. "Please help me."

"I will, but trust me when I tell you if you want this to be good, you have to slow down."

She gripped his shoulders tightly, believing him. He had the experience to make their union pleasurable. Nothing she'd read in the naughty books her aunt had given her talked about virgins and their experience. Everything she had read dealt with woman who wanted to improve the sex life they had in new and varied positions. Her aunt had advised the first time would hurt, but she'd also echoed Andrew's words to trust him. Miranda took a deep breath and released her thighs from around his hips, not realizing she had wound them around him.

"We need to slow down a bit. I had the whole evening planned to make this special for you."

She looked into his eyes. "Haven't you figured out yet that everything with you is special? I never imagined you could be so kind and romantic. You have made up tenfold for my years of sadness with weeks of joy."

"With you, it's simple. Miranda, I love you. A thousand times I've thought to tell you that. But this—now, seemed like the very best time. So I waited."

Tears blurred her vision. "You have shown me in everything you do that you care for me. It's why I met you at the altar today. If, for one second, I'd thought my feelings for you weren't reciprocated, I wouldn't have come."

"You love me?"

"Yes, and before you worry. I didn't love the earl. You were right; you *are* two different men. I admire the earl very much, but I love you, Andrew."

He caught her lips with his again, but softer, less frantic. Caressing her breast with one hand, he worked her thighs open with the other then slid it under her hip to lift her. He rubbed his hard cock against her once, twice, before positioning it at her opening and slipping in. He stopped at her maidenhead. She met his eyes and breathed deeply in preparation. Fear filled her. Yet, he waited, merely holding still above her. Unable to form a word, she nodded, and murmuring words of love against her mouth. He flexed his hips and surged.

A gasp caught in her throat. Pain filled her, tears formed, and, for a moment, she considered pushing him away.

Cupping her cheek, he caught her tears with the pad of his thumb and held her tight. "I am sorry— breathe with me, my love."

As he filled his lungs, so did she, and, together, they worked through the sharp hurt. Slowly, the pain faded, not completely, but enough to allow her to experience a strange, but not unpleasant, sensation of fullness.

"I am all right."

"That's all, no more pain. I promise." He slid out then back in.

Fear turned to marvel as what little pain remained lessened, to be replaced by the sensations of being full and part of more than simply herself. He eased up from her, never breaking eye contact, but brought his cock to the very entrance of her womanhood.

She squeezed, hoping to hold him in place. "Don't leave."

"I don't plan on it. Simply letting you feel your way."

Tentatively, she lifted her hips and, when he groaned, she did it again. She loved the feel of his muscles as they contracted with every thrust forward, only to relax again when he nearly left her.

He maneuvered his hand between them, working her nub. Bliss rocked through her. As he sped up, so did her desire to feel that ecstasy again.

Urging him on, she dug her heels into the bed until she screamed his name and let the tension go and waves of ecstasy passed through her. His hips pounded into her, and she held on for dear life, until he grunted and collapsed. Holding tight, she ran her fingers through his hair, and over his sweat-dampened back. Closeness like she had never imagined engulfed her, and she relished it. She imagined nothing sweeter in her life than this moment with him.

"I'm too heavy," he murmured.

Not minding the weight, she went to protest, but he had already rolled off of her, pulling her into his embrace. With a painstaking pace, he worked at the ties of her stays, loosening them enough that she could pull them over her head, along with her chemise. The petticoat soon followed, leaving she and Andrew gloriously naked, with the late day sun coming through the window bathing them in its warmth.

"Perhaps, if we should ever have a girl, we could name her Eve," Miranda said some hours later, her head resting on his chest, as he played with her hair.

"I think we will have to beat some other couples to the punch with that one then."

"What do you mean?"

"There are a few people I know who are giving thanks to the matchmaking abilities of Madame Eve."

Rubbing her bare leg up his, she lifted her head to gaze at him. "We should try hard to beat them then."

"I love the way you think." He rolled over, forcing her under him. "Now, tell me about these books your aunt gave you."

"What…but you already have plenty of experience in the bedchamber!"

"Perhaps you have a lesson or two to teach me." He curved over her, taking advantage as she hoped he would when she arched her neck for better access.

"You want me to show you?" her voice sounded far huskier than she'd ever imagined it could. And, although he was still leading her at the moment, she knew one day he would let her take control, but, for tonight, she loved how he made her feel, how much he felt for her. She'd never dreamed she would be loved as much as she loved, but he had proved he did. As his lips made a trail from her neck to her collarbone, all thoughts fled except the need to have this man in every way she could.

"Perhaps after a few more lessons myself," she agreed.

"How about I show you, then, my love?" Pulling the covers over them both, he blocked out the rest of world until only the two of them existed.

About the Author

Award-winning author Dominique Eastwick grew up a US Navy Brat, so if there was a naval base, that was probably home. She currently resides in North Carolina with her husband, two children, crazy lab and lazy cat.

Dominique's love of reading started when she was told to read *To Kill a Mockingbird* in high school—a book that opened her eyes to the joys of reading and entering into the world of the author. To this day she ranks this book as her favorite.

Book List

Strawberry Kisses

The Duke and the Virgin

The Marquis and the Mistress

Shifting Hearts

Healing His Soul's Mate

Infiltrating Her Pack